Praise for *I*

'A heart-warming, her<
written adventure will h
be engulfed by this wo........., ...-filled escapade, a
magical story that takes you from sea to sky on the
adventure of a lifetime ...'
KERRY MCLEAN – *broadcaster at BBC Radio Ulster.*

Praise for *Magical Masquerade*

'A rich, dream-like story full of pin-sharp pictures and
phantasmagorical creatures. The narration is deft, the
language is clean, clear and bright, and the style is
classical. Here is a work of which one can say, accurately
for once, that it exemplifies the virtues that one
associates with the golden age of children's fiction.'
CARLO GÉBLER – *author, playwright, creative writing
tutor, academic and former Bisto Merit Award-winner.*

'Claire Savage creates a sparkling fantasy world as rich
in charm and vibrancy as the best traditional fairy tales.
A pacey and engrossing tale told with flair, warmth and
charisma - a compelling new voice in children's fiction.'
FELICITY MCCALL – *YA author, playwright, arts
facilitator and former BBC journalist.*

Also by Claire Savage

Magical Masquerade

Phantom Phantasia

CLAIRE SAVAGE

First published in 2018 by CreateSpace
222 Old Wire Road, Columbia, SC 29172

ISBN-13: 978-1720843191
ISBN-10: 1720843198

www.clairesavagewriting.wordpress.com
Facebook: Claire Savage - Author
Twitter: @ClaireLSavage

Cover design by Design for Writers

Supported by the National Lottery through the Arts Council of Northern
Ireland.

LOTTERY FUNDED

For Joanne, James, Steven and Ryan.
(And Reuben, always).

Contents

Phantom Phantasia

'Phantom' – indefinable, obscure, shadow, spectre, spook, apparition, ghost. Something elusive.

'Phantasia' (Latin) – the mirror of imagination (Ref: Aristotle), the creative imagination, a capricious or fantastic idea, a genre of fiction or other artistic work characterised by fanciful or supernatural elements …

Conjure the setting, make it gleam -
Step inside what you think is a dream.
Once dusted with silver, festooned with light,
Now drowning in darkness, a kingdom in plight.
There's mystery and mayhem that shouldn't be there,
Skulking and hijinks to give you a scare.
The realm is unravelling, stitch by stitch,
Who knows how to save it – to reverse the glitch?
The answer, dear reader, may well surprise,
For it's not what you think and it will open your eyes.
To find the folk and restore the seams …
One must venture far, where wonder teems.
For many things lurk, down in 'The Deep',
Creatures that scuttle and quietly creep.
There are secrets, disguises, magic and more,
Forests of seaweed, a mountainous floor.
You might find a Bobbit, an eel, or a shark,
Watching and waiting, down in the dark.
Fish that are lanterns and snakes made of sand,
Corals and caves where adventures are planned.
Some folk are friendly and some folk are not,
There are places of marvel, others of rot.
Follow the sea and the mist and the moon,
Go fast as lightning – not a moment too soon.
You might find a girl, cunning and bold,
One who is clever and brave - so I'm told.
She's fighting for Fairyland, but will she succeed …?
… You'll discover the answer in the pages you read.

Chapter One
Return to the Realm

Fairyland was black and silver and full of shadows. Felicity shivered. This wasn't right. Her gaze swept over the unfamiliar landscape – all jagged edges and cloaked in darkness – searching for anything that might help her. But the fingernail of moon shed light only on strange shapes and unknown landmarks, so she would have to rely on instinct alone to reach her destination.

She clenched her fists, angry that the Fairy Realm had once again tricked her with its magic.

The crossover should have been easy – her mum and grandmother had held their Causeway stones and she had imagined herself back at the Mystical Mansion, so that's where they all should have ended up. Yet here Felicity was in the middle of nowhere while her mum and Granny Stone were who knew where in the realm. If they'd even made it to Fairyland, which she very much hoped they had.

She thought hard, knowing it was dangerous to linger out in the open for too long, especially when dark forces were likely still on the prowl. How much time had passed here and what had happened since she had last visited?

A screech split the silence and Felicity jumped. She told herself it was probably just an owl but nevertheless, a chill tip-toed down her spine. There might still be harpies on the loose.

To be fair, this was only her second time using her ability to travel between the realms, and her first time doing it from the human world to Fairyland without pebble magic, so perhaps it wasn't surprising that something had gone wrong.

Bob.

Felicity smacked her palm on her forehead. Of course. She'd been imagining the Mystical Mansion just as the Enchanter had told her to, but then she'd started thinking about her friend, assuming he would still be at the mansion.

He must have gone home and because she'd been thinking of too many different things, she'd ended up transporting herself somewhere in-between. She remembered that Bob lived near the Vanishing Lake, so perhaps she could find a sign pointing her in the right direction.

She only hoped there was a lake to be found, and that

it wasn't in its vanishing state. Then she really *would* be in trouble.

It was quiet and cool, a light breeze swirling Felicity's hair as she made up her mind. Keeping close to the hedgerow beside her she followed its length until it tailed off into nothing. The meagre moonlight revealed only hillocks ahead, with who knew what hidden amongst their peaks and troughs.

Yet she told herself she must not be far from Bob's home and that she had faced worse before in the Fairy Realm, so she hurried on, pulling her cloak tightly around her and keeping her eyes peeled for a brownie house – whatever that might happen to look like. She was concentrating so hard on finding it that it took Felicity quite by surprise when she ran into a figure rushing in the opposite direction. Or rather, *it* ran into her with a grunt and bounced back onto the hard ground.

'What business do you have running around in the dark at this hour?' a voice demanded, though it sounded a bit shaken.

Felicity, whose breath had been knocked clean out of her by the impact, grinned in the darkness.

She would know that voice anywhere.

'Bob.'

***

Tucked away safely in Bob's house, which hadn't been very far away in the end, Felicity relaxed at last as she shared a late supper with her friend. It was so good to see him again – and such a relief. They had waited until they were inside, then burst into conversation, their words all tumbling over one another as they each delivered their news.

'I've lost my mum and granny!'

'The Mystical Mansion is in lockdown—'

'Lockdown?'

'What do you mean, *lost*?'

'They had the Causeway stones but disappeared—'

'The Enchanter's been captured—'

'*What?!*' they said in unison, each with a dumbfounded look on their face.

Felicity nodded for Bob to speak. He took a deep breath.

'Since you've been gone, the witches and goblins have managed to move the Mystical Mansion to a mystery location – with the Enchanter and Hatchet and the rest of his staff trapped inside.

'They overpowered him, helped by the extra dark magic they've managed to obtain so far because of the forces leaking into the realm. He's powerful but, well, even the Enchanter can't defeat them alone now.'

'Why?' whispered Felicity, although she had a feeling she knew what the answer would be.

'They want his help to destroy the boundaries keeping the Fairy Realm safe from the other-worlds,' said Bob grimly. 'They don't *need* him to do it, but it would quicken the process, given his knowledge and powers. He has refused, of course. So far. But who knows what the witches might do to him to force his hand …'

Felicity swallowed.

'So, it isn't exactly good news to hear that his wife and daughter – and his granddaughter – are back in the realm, with two of them unaccounted for.'

'Do you think the witches will hunt us down?' asked Felicity, though she knew the answer to that as well.

'Yes,' said Bob. 'They have all sorts of reasons for wanting to snatch you - to harness the powers of you and your family; to hold you hostage so the Enchanter will do as they say ...' His face brightened then. 'But you're here with *me* and we can do our best to help!'

Felicity didn't know how they could possibly defeat the witches when the Enchanter couldn't, but she knew from her last adventure in the realm that the impossible wasn't always as impossible as it seemed.

'How?' she said, curious to hear Bob's plan. She *really* hoped he had a plan.

'Well, I know all of this because the Enchanter was able to get a message to me before the witches blocked communication with the mansion – magical or otherwise.'

He pulled a small scroll from his pocket, his hazelnut eyes shining. 'It lists all the folk who were spirited away by the pebbles *and* tells us what we need to do to rescue them. If we can do that, then it will heal the rifts caused in the boundaries when they were taken. *That* will stem the flow of the dark magic here and weaken the witches, buying the realm time to fight back. Never underestimate the power of restorative magic!'

Felicity was glad to hear they wouldn't have to face any witches directly – at least for now – but she had doubts all the same. 'Are you sure that's the best way for us to help?' she asked. 'Shouldn't we at least *try* to save the Enchanter, or fight against the witches here in some way?'

Bob shook his head. 'Not at all. If we restore the folk to Fairyland and repair the damage caused by the Enchanter's experiments when they were whisked away, then we start to reverse the process. We begin to restore the realm and make it whole again, which will help the Fairy King and Queen, who are amassing an army as we speak, to battle the dark magic and the witches. They can't spare soldiers for a rescue mission, but *we* can do that where we wouldn't be so good at combat.

'Fairyland is huge – much larger than you can imagine – so they need all their army here. Each of us must play our part in this battle, Felicity, and this is ours. Besides, we're the only ones in possession of the Enchanter's list of names.'

'What about my mum and grandmother?'

'You say they had Causeway stones?'

Felicity nodded.

'Then I suspect they were spirited directly to their home, as intended, in which case they may well be prisoners now too, I'm afraid. Or, there's a chance they might have ended up where the mansion used to be, or maybe they were returned to the weeping willow where they originally disappeared. But it's more likely the stones did their work and they are with the Enchanter.'

Neither of them suggested the other alternatives; that they might still be in the Human Realm, or somewhere else entirely.

'Now, catch me up on what's been happening with *you*.'

Felicity wasted little time in filling Bob in on what had happened since their last meeting.

On her return home to Granny Stone she had found, to her great surprise, a rather more informed Aurelia – or Audrey as Felicity knew her – waiting expectantly.

'The crows,' she told Bob, who listened intently.

'I thought they were either working for the witches or were just normal birds, but it turns out that my *granny*,' and her eyes sparkled as she said it, 'is an *enchantress*. An enchantress who also has crows which act as her personal messengers.'

'Or spies,' butted in Bob with a grin.

'Yes – or spies.' Felicity smiled. 'Well, if the witches have spies then it's only fair that those who fight for good have their own secret weapons! Anyway, they saw me disappear into the Fairy Realm, so she knew where I had gone, at least. She was still worried, but it helped that she knew something of what had happened.'

She paused. 'I'm eleven-and-three-quarters now, by the way - back in the human world – but still ten-and-three-quarter years old here … And no one realised I was missing back there as my granny glamoured their memories. To them, I never left at all. I don't know if *I'll* ever be able to do the same thing myself but, well, who knows?'

Despite the worry about her family, Felicity couldn't help feeling excitement bubbling up inside her at the words. She must have powers of *some* sort surely, being half of the Fairy Realm and half-human.

She could already cross freely between realms without the enchanted pebbles and her grandparents were *enchanters* after all, her mum too. Who knew what magic might be hidden inside her – or what she could learn?

Bob seemed to share her enthusiasm but a serious look flickered across his features. 'There's something I, er,

10

haven't told you yet about our imminent adventure,' he said, his eyes darting away from her face and then back again.

Felicity's heart skipped a beat and her mouth dried as she waited for him to continue.

'As well as the list of names the Enchanter sent, he also explained *how* we could track down exactly where they went without having to conduct any of his risky experiments.' The brownie paused. 'Just before he was captured, the Enchanter discovered the existence of a magical object which reveals where pebbles have taken folk, if you know their names to seek them out. An object not even the Pebble People themselves knew of, though I think there must have been rumours of it at one time, long lost to history. It's the ultimate "Pebble Reader", I suppose, as the Enchanter believes it can trace the cosmic trails left behind when folk disappear, picking them apart when the power of a fairy's name is used to work the magic.'

'Where is this object – and *what* is it?' breathed Felicity. Surely this was good news.

'That's the thing,' said Bob. 'Unfortunately, the Enchanter was captured before he could uncover the identity of this object. Also, if it really does exist, as he felt sure in the end that it did, then there's only one place it can be – at the home of the most light-fingered creature in the realm, who steals precious magic and objects and hides them away for himself ...'

Felicity gulped.

'Yes, I'm afraid we're headed for the Mountain of Lore – home to the Rhyming Riddler.'

Chapter Two

An Unexpected Guest

The last time Felicity had seen the Rhyming Riddler they'd parted on rather a sour note, so she couldn't help but shiver at the thought of seeking him out again. She hadn't told Bob and the others of the little magic man's parting rhyme, which hadn't exactly been friendly. She'd been warned not to underestimate his cunning and his wrath, so this was *not* good news.

'Are you sure that's where we have to go?'

Bob nodded. 'Looks very much like it.'

'But I thought – I thought you told me once that no one really knows where the Mountain of Lore is. So how are *we* supposed to find it?'

'Well, we will just have to find a way,' said Bob grimly. 'Though that will take time, which is why we'd need to leave right away. Portals are off-limits this time around, I'm afraid, as the witches have seized control of most of them and besides, they're becoming more and more dangerous to use, what with the rifts in Fairyland's borders. No, we will have to make this journey on foot!'

'We'll need supplies,' said Felicity. 'Lucky I remembered to bring my enchanted crockery along.' She grinned and held up the bag Wizard Mezra had given her on her last visit.

As she did so, however, a low rumble filled the air and Bob's house began to shake. Or, rather, the rows and rows of books on the shelves which covered the walls began to tremble, the blue-painted crockery on the sideboard began to clatter together like chattering teeth on a winter's day, and little puffs of soil drifted down upon them from their earthen surrounds.

Although the house was scooped out of the ground, the floor was made of stone. Felicity gasped as a corner of it suddenly erupted, sharp pieces of flint scattering across the room, which served as both kitchen and living area, and a figure popped out.

'Greetings!' said a cheery voice, at the same time as Bob exclaimed, with some dismay, 'My floor!'

'Clarity!' said Felicity with relief, recognising the little Pebble Person instantly. 'Thank goodness it's you. I thought for a minute that the witches and goblins had already found us.'

'My, my *floor*,' was all Bob could manage, going over to inspect the damage

'Hello Felicity,' said Clarity. 'I'm here to tell you that your mother and grandmother are safe and well and in our protection at the Rocky Valley. We found them under the old weeping willow after they crossed over and thought it best they didn't remain out in the open for very long, given all that's happened.'

Felicity let out a sigh of relief. 'So they *did* end up at the willow. Thank goodness they got back okay.'

'I've come to take you to them,' said Clarity.

'Oh—' Felicity stopped as a shriek sounded outside.

Bob paled. 'Scouts,' he whispered. 'Witches' spies, or maybe just monsters who answer to no one. There's no time to waste. Your family's safe Felicity and a detour now will only delay us. We can't risk it.'

'Detour? Are you going somewhere?' asked Clarity. 'I don't think that's wise. Seraphina and Aurelia are working with us to help the Enchanter. I'm to bring you back with me, Felicity, so you can assist and start to develop your powers under our watchful eyes. Who knows what you might be capable of? I'm sure that Bob can manage this other business on his own?'

Felicity hesitated. She did so want to see for herself that her mum and Granny Stone were safe, even if the Enchanter and Hatchet remained prisoners of the witches. On the other hand, they needed to find the Mountain of Lore – wherever it was – and try to heal Fairyland as soon as possible.

'I don't know …' she said. 'I think it would be best if I stayed with Bob. If mum and Granny Stone are safe with you then I'm not sure there's much I can help them with. Could you tell them I've got something important to do, but that I'll be back as soon as I can?'

Clarity pressed his lips together in annoyance and Felicity smiled back at him, hoping he wouldn't notice that it wasn't quite genuine.

Something didn't feel right. It could be nothing, but the Clarity *she* knew was kind and amiable and there was an aura around the Pebble Person standing before her that seemed wrong, somehow.

She couldn't put her finger on it. It certainly looked like her friend, but there was something missing in his manner and there was a coldness in his eyes that had never been there before.

'Why don't you come back with me and tell them in person?' asked Clarity. 'Then you can decide what to do next. It won't take long and they'll be so happy to see you.' He grabbed Felicity by the wrist with a cold, stony hand.

Now Felicity really knew something was off. The real Clarity would never resort to violence to get his way. She struggled to get free but the Pebble Person's grip only tightened.

'Here now – wait a minute! What are you doing?!' said Bob, turning away from his ruined floor at the commotion.

Clarity snarled in response and Felicity gasped as she detected the rich, sickly scent of cloves and spices on his breath. Back home, the aroma might be associated with cakes and Christmas, but in the Fairy Realm, Felicity knew it signalled only one thing.

Witches.

Her throat tightened as she stared into the eyes of the imposter before her. They were dull and lifeless and she realised she should have known at once that this wasn't the real Clarity.

How could she have been so easily fooled? She'd seen the shape of her kindly friend and failed to look beyond it. Tricked by yet another magical masquerade, and she was only just back in the kingdom!

She pulled her arm out of the spy's grasp at last, with a little help from Bob, who hurriedly began chanting as soon as she was freed.

He threw up his hands as he cast the spell, a mist gathering around them. It reminded Felicity of the magic the Enchanter had used in his mansion when the witches had surrounded him the last time she was here. She gaped at Bob.

'I've been practising!' he said with a wink, though his face was pale. 'It'll protect us – it's a magical barrier.'

'It might keep *me* out but it won't stop my *mis*tresses,' hissed a voice that was definitely not Clarity's.

17

Through the swirl of mist Felicity saw the pebble body melt like warm butter, the features sliding away last of all to pool on the floor. It bubbled and Bob and Felicity stared, transfixed, as the blob of what had a few seconds ago been a Pebble Person, seemed to soak into the stone.

'Wait!' cried Felicity. 'Who are you? And what about my mum and Granny Stone? You better not have harmed them!'

Her heart beat wildly as the last of the blob disappeared into the floor, her hope of an answer or some sort of explanation seemingly evaporating with it.

'A message for you, Fel – ic – it – y.' The voice was a whisper but yet somehow filled the room, the scent of spices now heavy in the air and making Felicity and Bob gag. 'Meddle with my mistresses and you will never see your family again. Know this – they are coming for you, one way or another, and when you least expect it.'

Silence engulfed the room after the final word was spoken and the air cleared of spice soon after. Keeping the misty barrier in place, Bob turned to Felicity.

'We must go *now*,' he said. 'That *thing* has only confirmed what we suspected. Your family has been captured by the witches, so we must hurry before they're forced to do something that could destroy Fairyland.'

Felicity looked at her friend, torn between wanting to save her family first and rescue the missing fairy folk. She knew, however, that looking for her family would see Fairyland sink further into ruin as they searched – and what if she and Bob were captured too? They could risk losing the realm to darkness altogether. She would just have to trust that her family could do what they needed to do and that she could do the same with Bob.

She thought of the innocent folk still trapped in any number of strange places beyond Fairyland's boundaries. What horrors might they be experiencing while they waited to be rescued? They couldn't just leave them there forever.

'Okay, let's go,' she said, her mouth pressed into a thin line. 'We don't have the power to fight the witches, do we?'

'No,' said her friend.

'Just checking. We *can* try to find the Mountain of Lore and heal the borders though. My family are bound to be working on an escape plan anyway so the best way for us to help is to find this – whatever it is that the Riddler owns - return the missing folk to the realm and start healing its borders. That will weaken the witches' powers, or at least distract them, helping the King and Queen's army do whatever needs to be done to defeat them. Have I left anything out?'

Bob grinned. 'I think that about covers it. Now, I've gathered what we need for the journey, which isn't much as we don't want to be weighed down with unnecessary items. We'd better get moving while it's still dark, especially with witchy servants, or whatever that was, on the loose. The fact they sent someone in their place to get you suggests that the witches are already feeling the strain of good versus evil. Let's hope we can help with that! We'll just have to take extra care to stay out of sight, away from watchful eyes.'

'Of witches and their crows,' said Felicity.

'Yes – and other spies.'

Felicity sighed. 'Is that even possible? They seem to be everywhere.'

'My dear Felicity,' said Bob, his features rising into a smile. 'With a little grit and determination, *anything* is possible – especially in Fairyland!'

Chapter Three
A Strange Catch

*A*nything is possible, especially in Fairyland.
Felicity kept repeating the words in her head as she followed Bob out into the darkness.

But *how* could the tasks ahead be possible, really, she fretted, when they had to find a place no one seemed to know the location of, steal an object they didn't know the identity of, and take it from under the very shrewd nose of that dratted Rhyming Riddler? Who, let's now forget, thought Felicity, was mad at her for not revealing the secret of the Causeway Stones, and for outwitting him at his own game. She shivered.

'Where exactly are we going?' she whispered to Bob. There were shrieks in the distance and she didn't fancy meeting the owners.

'I don't know, but I think we need to get as far away from here as possible,' said the brownie.

'The Mountain of Lore is well hidden, so first we travel beyond the familiar and then, hopefully, we'll find clues to its whereabouts thereafter.'

Felicity couldn't help thinking that this time yesterday

she'd been tucked up in her cosy bed at Granny Stone's, her mum and grandmother discussing their crossover to the realm for the hundredth time, it seemed. Their voices had bubbled beneath her, the steady flow of words comforting as she drifted off to sleep.

It had been surprisingly easy to get her mum out of 'The Institute'. She confessed that she had actually asked Felicity's father to take her there, making Felicity feel bad for having assumed her dad had done so against her mum's will. It had all seemed to happen so quickly at the time and no one had explained what was going on, so Felicity had made up her own narrative in the absence of any other.

Even her Granny Stone had kept schtum about the particulars, though Felicity realised now that her mum had asked her to do so, thinking she was protecting her daughter.

Her mother had eventually been ground down by the continual failure of her spells as she tried to reopen a path to Fairyland. So, she had hidden herself away to think and to try and come to terms with living forever in the Human Realm.

Once her mum heard that Felicity had been to the Fairy Realm and returned with a solution to their problem, however, she had simply discharged herself. There had been quite a lot of paperwork involved and various other things to be sorted out that Felicity didn't really know much about, but the main thing was that her mum had come home in what seemed like a flash and she had been very glad of it indeed.

'Easy as,' her mum had said with a wink. 'I checked myself in so I was allowed to check myself out again. I wasn't going to stay there forever anyway darling. I always meant to come home to you, just when I was in a better frame of mind.'

Felicity didn't know if that was completely true, as her mother had already been away for two years, but she'd missed her mum and was happy to have her back. She was her mother after all and Felicity knew that she cared about her. Both her parents did, in their own ways.

She bit back a yelp as Bob stopped abruptly in front of her and she walked clean into him. He grunted.

'Why are you stopping?' she hissed.

They'd left the Vanishing Lake behind and had entered a sort of wilderness filled with twisted gnarly trees and spiky bushes.

'I thought I saw something,' said Bob. 'A circle.'

'A what?'

'A blue circle. But it can't be – that hasn't been seen in years. And yet … perhaps it just might appear again at a time like this, when the realm is in such disarray and danger and needs urgently to be saved.'

'Bob, what on *earth* are you talking about?'

'A well – an enchanted well that will only permit you to locate it if it believes you really need it. That is, in times of great peril.'

'A wishing well?'

'Of sorts. Let's just say it has its own personality and sometimes grants wishes, sometimes grants answers. Sometimes, it does nothing at all. It's sacred and thought to have been enchanted by an ancient goddess of the glens.

'She was wronged in love and wept her joys and sorrows, her anger and pain, into the well and in so doing, granted it understanding of more than it should know. Her magic was powerful magic and a little of that leaked out of her and fed the waters of the well. It's said her spirit returned to it when she died.'

'Sounds creepy,' said Felicity.

'It's said to reveal itself as a blue circle of light on the ground,' said Bob. 'Then, once you approach it, the well itself forms – or so they say. I'm sure I saw something blue glittering on the ground over there. It so rarely reveals itself that you would be a fool indeed to ignore it. It could tell us how to find the Mountain of Lore!'

Felicity focused as hard as she could on the land around her, willing the well to materialise and hoping there were no witches, or other unsavoury creatures, prowling nearby.

'Bob—' she began, but the brownie gave a squeak of

delight at the same time, so she hurried over to him, almost scared to hope he had actually found what they were looking for. He had.

'Look,' he breathed in awe, pointing to a thin blue circle sparkling on the grass like a discarded crown.

The circle's circumference was about the size of a large manhole and as Bob and Felicity stared, the light began to pulse. The gentle lapping of water whispered at their ears and Felicity saw the blue circle was now fluid and flowing anti-clockwise. It sped round faster and faster, rising into an elegant whirlpool which splashed them with cool droplets before settling into the solid shape of a well.

The structure reached Felicity's middle – about head-height for Bob – its pale grey stones glowing with silver seams which indicated magic rather than cement. The wishing well had revealed itself.

'What now?' she whispered, hoping Bob would know how to work the well. If it was temperamental, like so many things in the realm, then they would have to take care in how they addressed it. 'Does it talk?'

Bob rubbed his chin. 'I don't honestly know. The stories go that folk who seek answers must speak their request into the silver bucket, then lower it and see what the well returns. Sometimes, it's nothing at all. But it's here, so it's certainly worth a try. We can both have a go. I'll ask for directions to the mysterious Mountain of Lore.'

Bob turned the handle at the side of the well, lowering

the small silver bucket dangling at the top. He grabbed it with both hands and whispered something inside, then sent it on down into the gaping darkness. After a while, a distant splash signalled that it had reached the bottom. Felicity and Bob both watched the well closely, waiting to see what would happen next.

A sharp tug came on the rope a few seconds later and Bob slowly drew the bucket up again. When it reached the top, the brownie pulled it to the well's edge and looked inside, a grin spreading over his face.

He pulled a piece of parchment tied tight with a red satin ribbon from the magical vessel and quickly un-scrolled it. 'A map. Basic, but a map all the same!'

Felicity studied it with him. The well appeared at the bottom and various landmarks were scattered across the page, but there was no route marked to tell them exactly where to go. At the top right-hand corner, however, a jagged peak had been drawn in red. The Mountain of Lore.

To reach it, they would have to choose their own path, but now at least they knew their options for the journey ahead.

'None of these places look very inviting,' said Bob nervously. 'But we'll seek shelter and look at this in more detail as soon as we can. Now, your turn, Felicity.'

Unsure of what to wish for, Felicity pulled the bucket

towards her and leaned her head into it. She wanted only to be fit for the task ahead and to succeed in their work. The words had left her lips almost before she realised she had spoken them.

'I wish for something that will help us save the Fairy Realm.'

She released the bucket and let it drop slowly down into the depths of the well. This time, however, it didn't reappear as quickly as before.

Felicity and Bob waited as the minutes ticked by and shadows flitted around them. The night was cool and quiet and yet Felicity knew there was every chance that someone, somewhere, was watching them. Now and again, a wail or a shriek split the air – from owl or otherworldly creature, Felicity knew not, but she *did* know one thing. It was time to go.

'Come on,' she said to Bob, after what felt like an age. 'I don't think it's coming up again. We have the map – that's enough to help us.'

'I don't think we should leave just yet,' said her friend. 'I'm sure the well always returns the bucket – be it empty or full. It wouldn't still be here if there wasn't something yet to reveal.'

'Why is it taking so long?' Felicity wanted to be patient but it was difficult to feel relaxed when she knew that things in the realm had a habit of tricking you with magic.

Just as she was about to tell Bob again that they really must go, the rope gave a jolt.

Immediately, she reached for the handle at the side of the well and tried to turn it, but it barely budged.

'Whatever's in the bucket isn't very light. Bob – can you help me?'

They both put their weight behind the handle and slowly, ever so slowly, wound it and wound it until Felicity saw something black and shiny appear at the rim of the enchanted well. They wound some more and then a thick black fringe appeared, chocolate-coloured eyes peering quizzically at Felicity as a button nose and a mouth forming a silent 'oh' appeared next. Felicity's own jaw dropped open.

'Sophie! What on earth are *you* doing here?!'

Chapter Four
Plots and Plans

Felicity stared at Sophie and Sophie stared right back at Felicity, a grin breaking across her face. Her legs were sticking out of the bucket, which had grown somewhat to accommodate its load, but not quite enough. The result was a girl stuffed rather messily inside, her arms and legs left to dangle where they would. If it hadn't been quite so surprising, Felicity would have laughed, but she found herself speechless.

'Well, hello to you too,' said her friend with a smirk. 'How are you Sophie, this dark, creepy night? Why, thanks for asking, Felicity my friend. I'm a bit bruised I think, because I seem to be stuffed into a magic bucket that's hanging over what I assume to be a magic well.

'Bit odd, isn't it? Well, since you ask, it *is*, but what's odder is that one minute I'm lying in bed dreaming myself off to sleep and the next, I've got my bum in a bucket, am winched up a well and come face-to-face with my, yet again, missing friend!

'How am I, you ask? Bit muddled really, but *delighted* to be here!' She wiggled her eyebrows, eyes twinkling mischievously.

Now Felicity did burst out laughing. She couldn't quite make sense of it but Sophie was here and her bubbly warmth was infectious and familiar and out of place in the realm all at the one time, and she couldn't help but see the funny side of the situation. Her friend really did look ridiculous suspended there above the well, her unicorn-slippered feet only adding to the comedy of it all.

'We'd better get her out of there before the well disappears,' said Bob.

Sophie squealed. 'A wee man! He's so cute! I mean, sorry, but you *are*. Felicity, is this … *Bob*?' Her eyes widened as the brownie helped Felicity pull the bucket to the edge of the well.

'Yes,' said Felicity, grabbing Sophie's arms as Bob steadied the bucket. 'It … is … *Bob*!' She staggered back as Sophie popped out like a cork. She fell into Felicity, who stumbled backwards onto the grass, Sophie landing beside her.

Bob looked down at the pair of them in amusement, his face luminescent in the moonlight. Behind him, the wishing well began to crumble away, brick by brick, dissolving slowly into the ground until only a sparkling blue circle remained. Then that, too, sunk into the soil, leaving the trio alone. They all stared at where it had been until a shriek jolted them from their stupor.

'Barn owl,' said Sophie.

'Maybe,' said Bob. 'But we'd best find cover just in case. There's more than barn owls loose tonight.'

'Awesome. So, where are we going then, Mr Bob the brownie? Felicity, you really should introduce us properly.'

'You're Sophie,' said Bob. 'Felicity's friend from the Human Realm.'

'Yes – and Bob's right,' said Felicity. 'I think we should get out of here. We can chat later Soph.'

'Can we go to your brownie house Bob?'

'We've just come from there,' said Felicity. 'Where *can* we go though?' She directed the question at Bob, who was already leading them onwards. Dark clouds scudded across the sky, blotting out the moon, for what it was tonight.

'We'll go to Butterkin's house – it isn't far from here,' said Bob. 'We should be safe enough there I hope. For now, anyway. We can study the map and make our plans for the journey ahead, and I'll see if I can conjure up some sort of concealment spell to make us a bit less conspicuous along the way. We can't know who's watching us, or when they will strike.'

'Creepy,' said Sophie. 'But also, *awesome.*'

***

Butterkin's home was a little further away than Felicity had hoped, as she was itching to speak properly with her friends and keen to find out more about what had happened to Sophie, but when they arrived at last it was certainly well worth the wait.

Built in a hollow with a few other houses scattered around it, the little stone structure felt welcoming despite its lack of dweller. Felicity was surprised it wasn't underground, as she knew by now that many fairy folk preferred to live under the surface, but she was also a bit glad, as she always felt a little trapped beneath the earth.

Inside, they found a small living room with a hearth that Felicity soon filled with flames. Granny Stone had taught her how to lay the fire at home and she often lit it in the winter evenings, so she got to work quickly to heat the little house.

'Let's see what there is to eat and then we'll talk,' said Bob, heading towards what Felicity assumed was the kitchen.

'What about my crockery?' she said, jiggling her bag. 'It will save us cooking and will be quicker. There probably isn't much in the way of food left here anyway, what with Butterkin gone for so long. Sorry ...' she tailed off, wishing she hadn't been **quite** so tactless

'That's okay. You're right, anyway,' said Bob. 'What'll we have then?'

Sophie's eyes almost popped out of her head as she watched Felicity summon food from the crockery Mezra had given her. They all agreed on a hearty stew with fresh crusty bread, and Felicity asked for lemonade for Sophie, milk for herself and elderberry juice for Bob. Dessert was rich chocolate brownies and ice cream.

Sophie tried not to stare at Bob as he ate his, but she couldn't resist. 'I'm sorry, but you're a brownie eating a *brownie*,' she said, giggling. 'It's a bit weird.'

Bob raised his eyebrows.

'It's what we call them at home,' said Felicity, elbowing Sophie. 'No offence.'

'None taken!' said Bob. 'At least I share my name with something gooey and chocolatey and delicious! Now, what about that map?'

Felicity and Sophie exchanged a look. They would catch up later. For now, planning their next move was more important, but Felicity couldn't help wondering where her school friend fitted into all of this. She'd asked the well for something that would help her and Bob, and Sophie was what it had presented so, bizarre as it was, she was obviously meant to be here. It was actually a bit of a relief, if she was being honest with herself.

Felicity had agonised about whether she should tell her

friend about her disappearance and her Fairyland adventuring when she'd returned home the last time. In the end, however, she'd just come out with it as, despite her Granny Stone's glamouring spell, Sophie, being her best friend, had still sensed Felicity's absence and seemed to smell the adventure off her when she returned, questioning her about what she had been up to. Felicity had also been desperate to share all that had happened with her friend anyway, and Sophie had accepted her account more readily than she could have imagined.

'What would you say if I told you that I'd been to Fairyland and back, and that I think I'm part-fairy?' she'd asked.

'I would say,' said Sophie slowly, eyes gleaming with excitement, 'that you've always been a little unusual, so this could very well make sense. Tell me more and make it quick!'

And so, she had. It had been a relief to share her story and Felicity had felt bad slipping back to the realm this time around without trying to take Sophie with her. Her friend had beseeched her to let her tag along but Felicity's mum and Granny Stone had forbidden it and had been more than a little worried that she'd spoken to Sophie about her family secret. Felicity trusted Sophie, however, and she couldn't wait to show her the realm and introduce her to Hatchet and the Enchanter – if they were able to free them, that was.

Bob spread the map on the table and they studied it closely. 'Hmm,' he rubbed his chin. 'There certainly doesn't seem to be a straightforward way to reach the Riddler but then, it was never going to be easy, was it?'

'The Whispering Woods,' said Sophie, poking at the map.

'The Bubbling Swamp, The Dark Forest. No, it doesn't sound like an easy journey.' Felicity grimaced.

'Without specific directions to follow we'll have to choose our own route,' said Bob, 'the most direct way appearing to be through the Whispering Woods and the Dark Forest, then on to whatever *that* is surrounding the Mountain of Lore.' He pointed on the map. 'I doubt that it's just sitting pretty on the other side of the forest for anyone to approach. We should assume the Riddler will have some added protection or concealment around his lair.

'Also, there will be many challenges along the way, for all sorts of creatures will be lurking – even more than usual, what with Fairyland's damaged borders.'

'But at least we have some idea of how to get there now,' said Felicity. 'If only we knew what we were looking *for*. Hopefully we can find out along the way. There's bound to be some sort of spell we can do, surely, that will help identify this mysterious magical object?'

'Ooh – are we going to get to do spells? Brilliant. Can you do spells yet Felicity?'

Felicity smiled at Sophie. 'I don't think so – I mean, no, I can't. Though I did read one out before and it worked on the witches. Is there anything in your books, Bob?'

'There are spells you can use to reveal identities, but none I've found so far have helped,' said the brownie. 'It's not that they don't *work* necessarily, rather that they may require more intricate spell-casting than I can manage, to give us the answer we seek. It's also difficult when we don't know what this object looks like.'

They spent the next few hours checking Butterkin's few spell books and plotting their route on the map. They agreed it was best to rest for now, Bob having cast a simple concealment spell around the house to shield them from any spies, though it wouldn't stand up to scrutiny, should a powerful witch decide to pay a visit, he'd pointed out. 'We'll just have to hope they're all too busy concocting their evil plans,' he said with a wry smile.

Felicity found Sophie some clean clothes from Butterkin's wardrobe – an assortment of brown trousers, tunic, boots and jacket, which Bob altered with a little magic to make them fit. Then she asked her crockery for some hot chocolate before bed and the pair exchanged stories while Bob half-listened, half-read the spell books again, in case he might have missed something.

'I can't believe I'm actually here in Fairyland,' said Sophie. 'Even though you told me about it, it's hard to really believe it's real.'

'And you haven't even seen very much yet, in the dark,' laughed Felicity. 'It's dangerous for humans though – even more than usual since the Enchanter's experiments - and now the witches and goblins are making things worse with their dark magic.'

'Witches and goblins.' Sophie shook her head in wonder. 'The stuff of fairy tales - and we're actually talking about them because they're really real and in the same world as us. I sort of want to see them but I also sort of don't. Creepy creatures.'

'And dangerous. Goblins *eat* human flesh, don't forget.'

'I *had* forgotten, but thanks for reminding me!' Sophie wrinkled her nose in disgust.

After telling her what had occurred so far that night, Felicity asked, 'So, what happened to you at home Soph?'

'Not much to tell really. As I said, I was in bed, about to drift off to sleep, when I felt cold all of a sudden, so I got up to check the window was closed and put my slippers on to warm up. Next thing I knew, I was sitting in a magic bucket in a magic well. It was pitch dark so I saw nothing until you yanked me up.'

'Your parents will worry when they realise you've gone.'

'I know. I don't suppose you can cast a – what was it your granny did – a glamour? Can you do that to them from here?'

''Fraid not,' said Felicity glumly. 'Unless – Bob?'

He shook his head sadly.

'You can go home now if you want Soph,' said Felicity. 'I can give you a Causeway stone. You don't have to come with us.'

'What? And miss the adventure of my *life*?!' said Sophie. 'No way! We'll just have to find this Mountain of Lore, complete the quest and get me home as soon as we can. You outwitted this Riddler before, Felicity, so I'm sure we three can do it again.'

Felicity smiled with more confidence than she felt. She just hoped that her friend was right.

Chapter Five
River of Tears

'D o you think we're being watched right now?' said Sophie as they wolfed down eggs and toast the next morning.

'They can't have eyes on us all the time, but I have no doubt they'll try their best,' said Bob, in between swallows of nettle tea. 'The witches may be working elsewhere but they have spies aplenty, which is why we need to be careful.'

'Just keep a lookout for crows and other suspicious eyes,' said Felicity. 'And don't ignore the prickle that might appear on the back of your neck, as it probably means you're being watched!'

Sophie shivered. 'Message received. We are like fugitives on the run – hunted by witchy folk and their strange familiars. Who is friend? Who is foe? Nobody knows.'

Felicity rolled her eyes, mouth tugging into a smile nevertheless. 'You make it sound like a trailer for a film.'

Sophie grinned at her.

It felt good having her friend here, but Felicity couldn't shake off the feeling of unease she had that there might be eyes anywhere as they made their way to the Mountain of Lore - unfriendly eyes trained on them and specifically on *her*. They would no doubt be watching to see if any of her powers came to light and probably planned to capture her, or steal the object they sought from the Riddler. It wasn't going to be easy but then, what expedition in the Fairy Realm ever was?

They left Butterkin's as sunrise started eating the shadows of night, leaving long before anyone from the neighbouring houses was up and about. Felicity spotted a wooden sign with the words 'Bluebird Hollow' painted on it in cornflower blue, then she slipped after the others, leaving the last trace of familiarity and safety behind.

Felicity had already been in Witch Wood and the Enchanted Forest, so she wondered what surprises lurked in the Whispering Woods. She knew the trees talked to one another, but she was fairly certain there would be more than that to worry about. She was just grateful they weren't going to the Bubbling Swamp and that Bob had been able to cast a concealment spell around them. It was quite basic, which he had apologised for, but it would distract the eye from them, should they meet anyone, though it wouldn't last long into their journey

'I'm afraid my magic isn't strong enough to sustain it,' said Bob, 'and I don't have any more supplies to recast it, as I used them up concealing us at Butterkin's house.'

'We'll just have to use our wit to, er, outwit the witches and ghouls then,' said Sophie. 'Actually, *will* there be ghouls?' She pulled a face. 'I hope not!'

They walked on into the morning, each lost in their own thoughts. It was a comfortable silence that was nevertheless tinged with unease at what might lie ahead. Fairyland slowly awakened around them, unfurling like a flower as the sun stirred her from slumber. Birds chirruped, unseen, in the hedgerows, which were strung with lacy webs that winked as light glanced off the dewdrops caught on the silken traps.

Although it was now spring in the Human Realm one year on since Felicity's first journey into Fairyland, time in the Fairy Realm ambled on more slowly. As a result, they were travelling in the beginning of the fairy summer Felicity thought she might have missed after leaving. Bob explained, however, that the darkness infecting Fairyland was upsetting the seasons, so summer was warping into winter more and more every day. Indeed, the grass felt crisp underfoot, lightly coated with a frost that was out of sync with the season.

The trio stopped briefly mid-morning to snack on warm pancakes - drizzled with honey for Bob, smeared with chocolate for Felicity and dusted with sugar and cinnamon for Sophie. Bob looked a little surprised by Sophie's choice, but she just grinned and licked the sugar off her fingertips. Felicity laughed. Her friend enjoyed food combinations that some – okay, *most* people – found strange. Bob would have to get used to seeing odder eating habits than *that* by the time they were through with their adventures.

They packed up and spent the rest of the day meandering through a landscape which seemed to alter around every bend. Small grassy slopes sprouting buttercups and pale pink flowers that swayed in the breeze gave way to stubbly soil strewn with rocks, and barren, except for a few spiky thistles here and there. Beyond that, they came upon a meadow with a stream gurgling through it, long-limbed creatures with thin tails and feathery wings leapfrogging across the tall grasses and wildflowers, their faces sharpened to a point.

Sophie's eyes widened when she saw them. 'I don't think you'll find *these* in my natural history books! What on earth are they?'

'Spindlebies,' said Bob. 'I wouldn't get in their way though. They pinch and bite when they can – and just for the fun of it! Harmless enough, but unpleasant creatures all the same.'

The brownie had no sooner uttered the words when he gave a yelp. 'Ow!'

Snickers floated up from the meadow and Sophie and Felicity tried to hide their grins.

'That told *you* anyway!' said Sophie.

Other than the Spindlebies and some passing wildlife, Fairyland threw no further surprises at the trio as they made their way onwards to the Whispering Woods. They weren't entirely comforted by the fact, however, and when night fell, they took shelter in a crevice almost big enough to be a cave, at the side of a river that Bob told them was called the River of Tears.

'So it isn't fresh water?' asked Felicity.

'Yes and no,' said Bob. 'The "tears" that form the river are said to flow from the Weeping Wand – a tree so tall and so thin and so full of magic that it weeps water as pure as rain. Purer, in fact. It is an ancient tree that is said to be the life-giver of all the trees in Fairyland – the living liquid that bleeds from it comes from millions or more tiny cuts in its bark, which its very own branches have inflicted, in order to give sustenance to the root systems of the realm.

'It is one of our own legends, or myths, if you like, for it is another of these mysterious appendages of Fairyland that none could direct you to, but most have heard of. Some say it's now so thin it's invisible, yet still it sustains.

'The River of Tears mixes with the other streams and rivers of the realm, of course, but it's this river which gets the name it has because it flows around the Whispering

Woods. Perhaps the Weeping Wand dwells within; perhaps not. The Whispering Woods have more of a reputation for trickery and for talkative trees than elsewhere in Fairyland though, so some folk think their boldness comes from being close to the source.'

'Talkative trees,' mused Sophie. 'Can't wait! The budding botanist in me - no pun intended - has a *load* of questions for those guys.'

'You'll be lucky if you can manage to decipher what they say.' said Bob.

Felicity let their voices fade into the background as she inspected their hidey-hole. It was better shelter than they had hoped for in many ways, but still, she felt uneasy about the gaping entrance, which was big enough for all manner of creatures to get through. They were as far back into the space as they could go, however, where the rock walls tapered to a point. Bob had made a magic, smokeless fire for them and 'bed' would have to be their coats and cloaks.

There was something unusual happening with the rock beside Felicity, however – she was sure of it. In the firelight, it seemed to be rippling and slowly starting to rearrange itself. When she allowed herself to blink, Felicity sucked in a breath, for in that split second, letters had appeared.

Working to free your family.

Fear not, Felicity.

Cobble.

'Bob!'

Bob and Sophie's heads snapped towards her. Felicity just pointed.

'Coool,' Sophie poked at the wall as the letters sunk back into the rock. 'Oops. I didn't mean to—'

'It's okay,' said Felicity. 'Cobble wouldn't have left them there for someone else to find. He probably sensed they'd been read and the message delivered.' She breathed out slowly. 'With the Pebble People *and* the combined powers of the Enchanter, my mum and Granny Stone, surely they'll find a way to escape the witches? It helps a lot knowing my family aren't alone in all of this.'

She'd kept the fear that was gnawing away at her hidden as best she could from Bob and Sophie up until now, but Felicity's family had been on her mind ever since she'd arrived back in Fairyland and found herself alone – again. Cobble's message was some reassurance. She knew they three were no match for the witches and goblins with their increasing army of ghouls, but she'd still felt guilty about doing nothing to help them.

'They'll work together to get free – I'm sure of it,' said Bob. 'No one else can do what we're doing though, Felicity, it's only us who know of the Enchanter's work and what must be done, and it will sew the final crucial stitches needed to mend the realm if we can find this object, retrieve the missing fairy folk and in so doing, heal the borders. We're doing our bit, and it won't be easy, but we have every faith in you, don't we Sophie?' He elbowed Sophie, who squeaked out a 'Yes!'

Felicity felt her resolve strengthen again at her friends' words. They could do this – she *knew* they could – otherwise why had they been brought together? And she knew from her previous visit that she somehow affected Fairyland, though she had no idea why, so perhaps this time around *it* would affect her right back and reveal what powers – if any – lay within her.

'Well,' she said, a smile inching across her face. 'We *do* have a great team here, so how could we possibly fail? And I don't mind saying that I'm looking forward to outwitting the Rhyming Riddler again.'

They chatted on into the night, before Bob took first watch and the girls fell asleep. Felicity had hoped for the deep, dreamless sleep that Sophie seemed to have succumbed to, but it wasn't to be.

Instead, her dreams were filled with strange creatures the like of which she'd never seen before, beckoning her onwards into somewhere cold and dark and hidden. It was somewhere at the very heart of the world, where treasures - and danger - lay waiting to be found.

Chapter Six
The Whispering Woods

The Whispering Woods stood dark and defiant before them, revealing no hint at what lay within. All that separated Felicity, Bob and Sophie from the trees was a bridge resplendent with colour and made from a material that Felicity knew would never be found in the Human Realm.

'Dragonscale Bridge,' said Bob. 'And beyond it, well, who knows? I've never crossed it! We stay close to home, myself and Butterkin. Or at least, we used to …'

Felicity studied the bridge. It was low and long, curving over the River of Tears in a gentle arc and leaving little room underneath for any river traffic. The bridge glimmered in the morning light, a fusion of pastel pinks and purples, and of amber, emerald and gold.

Streaks of silver also shone across the scales, which were arranged as regimentally as if they were on a dragon itself – half-moons layered neatly on top of one another, overlapping all the way to the other side.

It was simple in design, but very impressive.

'Off to the Whispering Woods then,' she said.

Sophie's eyes shone with excitement while Bob looked rather serious. Felicity just hoped their efforts would pay off and that they would find Butterkin - and everyone else - safe and sound.

They crossed the bridge quickly, slipping now and again on the scales. They felt the change as soon as they reached the other side. The air hung heavy around them and made Felicity's skin prickle, as if she was being watched.

'Do you feel – weird?' said Sophie. 'As if you're in somebody's line of fire?'

'Yes, something like that.' Felicity turned towards the trees. 'Let's get out of the open and through these woods as quickly as we can. Is there anything else we should know about the Whispering Woods before we go in Bob?'

'Just keep your wits about you, move quickly and look out for the usual fairy rings and mounds. I'm not entirely sure who else dwells within, but be prepared to run if we encounter anything untoward. No questions asked.'

'I still have my ring from last time,' said Felicity. 'But it will only glamour the person wearing it. Here,' she fished in her bag and withdrew the ring, handing it to Sophie. 'Bob has some magic and, well, perhaps I do too, somewhere inside me. But it's my fault you're here Sophie and I can't let anything happen to you, so I'd feel better if you had it. Please,' she added, as Sophie shook her head.

'You don't *know* that you have magic, Felicity, and if you do, you need to find it first and then work out how to use it. You're as much at risk as I am – and it's not *your* fault that I'm here, or your responsibility to keep me safe. We'll just all look out for each other, okay?'

'Okay,' said Felicity. 'But please, Soph, take the ring.'

Sophie sighed, then took the enchanted jewellery and pocketed it. Felicity squeezed her friend's arm in thanks.

'Let's just keep up a steady pace until we find somewhere that looks safe to stop for rest and food,' said Bob. 'Best not to linger in here if possible though.'

The Whispering Woods were cool and shady, sunlight dappling on the ground before them, shadows dancing in and out of their vision as they walked abreast of one another. Felicity wasn't as talented a naturalist as Sophie, but even she could identify oak trees by now, along with hawthorn and ash. Fir trees were easy to spot, of course, and Sophie pointed out elms, hazel and birch as they walked. There really did seem to be every species of tree in the woods and they seemed to grow closer together the further in amongst them the three friends went.

It was eerily quiet, until the whispering started.

At first, Felicity dismissed the noise as the breeze humming through the branches splayed above and around them, but as it grew louder she knew it was the trees themselves talking - whispering in a language she knew was one none of them could speak or understand.

It reminded her of the time she'd moved schools – before she made friends with Sophie – when the whispers of her classmates and other pupils followed her like a wasp around a picnic. Of course, at school, she had been able to understand every word. The whispers had become a constant hum of background noise for a time, something she couldn't quite shake off, but best ignored, as acknowledgement only seemed to further kindle the fire. She'd felt all those eyes upon her, however, as she did now, the voices seeping into her consciousness regardless.

Felicity shivered. It wasn't a nice feeling and she wasn't going to let trees - even fairy trees - intimidate her. After all, once everyone at school had gotten to know her a bit better - when she made friends with Sophie and a few others and became less of a curiosity and part of the fabric of the place - the whispers had quietened, diluted and eventually, ebbed away until one day, Felicity realised they had disappeared completely.

So, she decided to speed up the process now and get friendly with these gossiping trees.

'I'm sure you're wondering who we three are and why we're wandering through your woods,' she said clearly, looking around at the trees.

Bob threw her a horrified look, while Sophie just stared at her as if she'd gone mad. Perhaps she should have explained her plan first, but she'd started now, so she might as well keep going.

'Well, *I'm* Felicity Stone and these are my friends - Bob, the brownie, and Sophie Riley. We just need to get through here as quickly as possible, so we can, er …' She paused. She thought it better not to reveal where exactly they were headed, but surely mentioning the Dark Forest was okay?

'We're going to the Dark Forest,' she said quickly, 'so if there's any way you can help us find it, or at least, be friends to us along the way, then we'd be very grateful. We love nature. Sophie, especially, knows a lot about trees.'

Sophie nodded slowly at this, raising her eyebrows at Felicity.

Something had happened, however. They all sensed it. The whispering had eased while Felicity was speaking and now that she'd stopped, not a breath stirred. Then, as if a ferocious gust of wind had whirled through the woods, the trees shook their branches in what seemed like agitation.

'Now look what you've done,' said Sophie.

'It was a risky plan,' said Bob. 'Trees are temperamental creatures and these ones might not take

51

very kindly to what you just said – or even to being directly addressed. Perhaps I should have mentioned that before – don't talk to the trees.'

'Wait - I think they're trying to tell us something,' said Felicity. She looked at Bob. 'I don't suppose you speak "tree" by any chance?'

The brownie shook his head. 'Their language is ancient and has evolved so much over the centuries that it's a hotchpotch of all kinds of strange earthy dialects and languages. Few can speak it or understand it. In other parts of the realm some of the trees are more easily understood, but here, we're in a place where the old ways linger still.'

Felicity frowned. She was sure she felt a connection with this living army around her. She couldn't explain it – it was just a feeling that she had. Her grandmother always told her to follow her gut, however, and so, she decided to do just that. She pressed her palm against the rough, flaky bark of the nearest tree. At once, a flurry of whispering rose up around them. Bob and Sophie stopped in their tracks.

'Wait.' Felicity waved her other hand at them. She put her ear to the trunk, closed her eyes, and listened.

At first, it reminded her of the rich sound of the ocean which spoke when she put her ear to seashells back at home. But after a few moments, the rush of noise became something more like babble – a torrent of foreign mutterings, clicks, hisses and stops that she couldn't understand. And yet – these too seemed to rearrange themselves into something more comprehensible, fracturing into separate voices until Felicity could pick out different personalities – trees – conversing.

She knew she had never heard the language before and yet, the more she listened to it, the more she started to get the sense of the shape of it and the meaning it conveyed.

And the trees sensed it.

They started talking to her in their hissing, whispering way, all speaking at once so it was difficult to catch their messages. It became apparent, however, that these ancient beings were indignant at the threesome's invasion into the woods, and at Felicity's intrusion into their conversation. There was also some resentment that she could follow their meaning. Suspicion hung around the edges of their words and yet in some, Felicity also sensed wonder and a little hint of welcome. She closed her eyes and tried to focus in on what they were saying, but only snippets came through, with the steady pulse of something else. It felt like danger.

'Down in the dark, down in the dark,' one tree chanted.

'Hidden and deep – oh so deep,' said another.

'What? The forest?' Felicity asked them, batting Bob or Sophie away as one of them grabbed her arm.

'Swirly-whirly, silly girly,' mocked another, and Felicity felt anger rise up inside her. She opened her eyes at another insistent tug on her arm and found herself looking at an anxious Bob.

'Can you understand them?' he asked, incredulous. 'You do, don't you? But tell me later, for I think we have a problem that needs sorted out first.'

'Yes,' gulped Sophie, eyes flicking nervously under her thick fringe. 'Dark, prickly problems in the shape of creepy, spiky little elves. They're *watching* us,' she whispered.

Felicity looked about them and saw shadows moving through the trees above, glints of eyeballs trained on the quarry below. Them.

'What do we do?'

'Remain calm and gather ourselves,' said Bob, looking them each in the eye. 'And when I say "run", run as fast as you possibly can and *don't* look back. Dark Elves distract their prey by darting around them and flitting to and fro, so you only ever catch a glimpse of them from the corner of your eye. It disorients you and makes you question what you're seeing, until you think yourself foolish and stop. That's when they pounce.'

'Okaay ... Glad we cleared *that* up!' said Sophie, looking horrified. 'Run fast and don't forget we've seen the wee creeps. Got it.'

'Got it,' said Felicity.

Bob nodded as the shadows gathered around them and Felicity tried to ignore the sly laughter of the trees as the brownie counted down. 'Three, two, one – *run!*'

They ran.

Bolting through the woods, the trio dodged outstretched branches that tried to entangle them, vaulting over protruding roots as they felt sharp fingernails scratch at their skin, the trees so close together now that it was like weaving through a living monster of an obstacle course. Shrieks followed in their wake as the elves gave chase, relishing the hunt, while Felicity, Bob and Sophie gulped down the stagnant air of the ancient woods.

An almighty crunch and a bloodcurdling scream stopped them in their tracks.

The skittering above them ceased immediately and the shadows melted away as Felicity felt the ground tremble. She put her ear to the trunk next to her and it whispered back.

'The Gobblers are here.'

Chapter Seven
Gobblers

The tree's words made Felicity's stomach somersault. Whatever the Gobblers were, they didn't sound good. Something had certainly spooked the Dark Elves, however, and she imagined it would have to be very dangerous indeed to do that.

'*Gobblers?*' she hissed at Bob. 'Ring a bell?'

'No, but I'd wager they're not something we want to hang around for,' said the brownie.

'Don't you know all of the creatures in the realm?' said Sophie.

'Not at all. There are always creatures hidden away, or metamorphosing, or shape-shifting; creatures that are ancient and unseen; fabled folk and new folk. Also, sometimes we fairy folk call things by different names, so you can never be quite sure if you're talking about the same thing.'

'Doesn't that get just a bit confusing?' asked Sophie.

Felicity glanced around, cold creeping into her bones.

Silence had fallen and she didn't like it, especially as the last thing they'd heard had sounded very much like somebody meeting a grisly end.

'I suppose we're still discovering new plants and animals, even back home,' Sophie continued, her voice dropping to a whisper. 'Must be even harder to keep track of what's what when magic is involved.'

They stood huddled together under the trees, which had hushed now completely. Unconsciously, they all seemed to have decided to ignore Bob's previous warning to run at the first sign of danger, and instead, waited like deer which had sensed a predator and were biding their time to bolt.

Felicity felt frozen to the spot, yet there was fire coursing through her. She was ready to run when the time came – or do what was necessary to escape these Gobblers. If Fairyland had taught her anything so far, it was that hope was never beyond reach and not everything was as it seemed. She tensed at the sound of rustling in the undergrowth, felt her heart miss a beat as something emerged – slowly.

'Oh!' said Sophie. 'It's so cute!'

'*What?!*' Felicity hissed, stepping backwards, her eyes narrowing. 'How is *that* cute?'

Sophie looked at her in confusion.

'You're telling me that fluffy isn't cute? Nope – I'm not buying it!'

'Wait a minute. What exactly do you see?'

'Um, what *you* see? A cute-as-pie something or other. True, it looks a bit unusual but it's still so cute! Big eyes, sticky-out ears - about the size of a small dog.'

'Well, *I* see a scaly thing with a huge mouth that wouldn't look out of place in the land of dinosaurs,' said Felicity. 'Bob?'

'I'm afraid I don't see anything,' said the brownie, who was looking more worried by the second. 'But I think it's time for us to run again.'

'Agreed. Sophie, whatever you're seeing must be a glamour. It's trying to trick us and confuse us. No matter what its true form is, if it's enough to scare away Dark Elves, then it should be enough to get us moving too. Just trust me.'

Sophie seemed about to object, but edged slowly away from the creature with Bob and Felicity as it moved towards them, others emerging behind it. Felicity saw gleaming orange eyes watching them intently, huge slobbering mouths with thick rubbery lips opening to reveal rows and rows of yellow jagged teeth, as the creatures' tongues tried to contain their drooling.

Scales covered their legs and faces and what Felicity could see of the rest of their bodies, but she could barely tear her gaze away from those massive mouths. Yes, these were most certainly the Gobblers. The question was – why was *she* the only one seeing them in their true form? The second question was whether they could outrun them. There was only one way to find out.

The Gobblers had stopped, and were still watching and salivating as if the outcome of their situation was obvious.

'Now!' grunted Bob.

The three friends sprinted away from the slavering beasts, dodging trees that remained silent as they passed, so all Felicity could hear was the pounding of their feet on the ground and their ragged breaths. She quickly realised what was missing was the sound of the Gobblers in pursuit. She was bringing up the rear, Sophie ahead of her and Bob up front, so she risked a glance behind. No one was following.

'Guys,' she gasped. 'Where have they gone?'

Sophie and Bob skidded to a halt, Felicity bumping into Sophie with a grunt.

'Okay, now I'm *really* freaked out,' said Sophie, eyes wide. 'Unless … If I know animals – and I do, whether they're fairy or not – then I can tell you now that they can have very clever ways of hunting. For instance, dolphins have been known to round up fish, surrounding them completely before they take a bite. Ah.'

'It would seem that we are the fish in this scenario,' said Bob. 'And here are our "dolphins",' he added, as the Gobblers re-emerged around them. They were now in the centre of a circle of very hungry-looking beasts and Felicity tried frantically to think of an escape plan as they drew ever closer.

***

The friends had been out-manoeuvred by the Gobblers, who were obviously cleverer than they looked, thought Felicity glumly. They were trapped and she heard the trees start up their whispering again, though she didn't feel like hearing whatever it was they were saying.

The Gobblers now filled the gaps between the trees around them, eyes glowing with greed, mouths dripping saliva. Felicity, Bob and Sophie stood back-to-back so each faced outwards towards the creatures.

'What now?' asked Sophie.

'The protective barrier will buy us a little time,' said Bob, as the familiar mist swirled up around them, obscuring the view of the slavering Gobblers. 'But I think we can safely assume that the concealment spell ran its course a while ago, and to be honest, I'm not quite sure how long this force-field will shield us from these hideous creatures – if at all. There's a different kind of magic lacing these woods and I sense that both it and the creatures within it are stronger as a result.'

'What about climbing the trees?' said Felicity.

'Didn't seem to help the Dark Elves,' said Sophie.

'But we have to try something! The Gobblers will have lost sight of us with this mist so they won't know what we're up to. There's always a way – there has to be. Let's just try it.'

With nothing else for it, the trio grabbed the branches of the nearest tree and pulled themselves upwards, one-by-one. It was a strange sort of a tree – a magical mixture of evergreen and deciduous which helped to conceal them further.

Below, the mist swirled as Bob left it lingering to fool the Gobblers into thinking they were still somewhere inside it.

Felicity risked a glance down and saw the creatures were now sniffing around it. She stifled a gasp as the first Gobbler leapt into the mist and disappeared. It wasn't going to hold them back at all. It was a good job they had climbed when they had, she thought grimly, or else they would have been torn limb from limb by now. She shivered and climbed higher - and faster.

From below there now rose growls and snapping sounds, followed by claws scraping bark. The Gobblers were in pursuit.

'Faster,' Felicity urged Bob and Sophie.

The tree didn't appear to be thinning out in any way, which helped, though Felicity wondered how high up it actually went. More importantly, did it lead to anywhere else? After all, this *was* Fairyland so you never knew where you might end up. On the other hand, it could just go on forever. She was beginning to feel tired, her arms and legs growing heavy.

'You'll never outrun them, or should I say, out*climb* them,' whispered a voice at her ear.

Felicity jumped, scrabbling for hold on the tree as she almost fell. 'Who said that?' She could see no one.

'You might call me your saving grace, your shining knight, your … fairy godmother of a sorts, my dear. Well, you might – if I decide to help you.'

'Why would you do that?' Felicity puffed, reaching for another branch and trying to catch up with Bob and Sophie. Below, she heard claws grappling against the trunk – a lot closer than she would have liked.

'Well – do you agree?'

'To what?'

'To my assisting you in your hour – or should I say *moment* – of need?'

'Who *are* you? And at what cost will you "help us," for I know there's bound to be *some* catch to this.'

The voice tutted, then sighed. 'Do you think I wish to *trick* you?' it mocked. 'That's a risk you'll just have to take, isn't it? Hark at them below. Do you feel their breath? Do you smell it?'

Felicity *could* smell something foul and meaty in the air and she knew it was the Gobblers' breath. She yelped as she looked down and saw glowing eyes just a few metres behind her. The Gobbler snorted and lunged.

They were out of time.

'Okay! Help us – help us all three, please,' she said. 'I trust you. But please – do it *now!*'

Felicity felt claws scrape against her leg as the Gobbler pinned her to the tree trunk, its hot, rancid breath filling her nostrils. She screamed and tried to kick it off just as its other front paw came rushing towards her, claws deadly and sharp as ice picks racing towards her face.

She closed her eyes. She couldn't move. All she could do was wait for this thing to shred her and devour her as it had the Dark Elves, and no doubt countless other creatures. How could she have let this happen? What had she led Bob and Sophie into?

Felicity felt tears prickle. What was taking so long? Perhaps the Gobblers liked to play with their food first, but they struck her more as beasts that simply devoured their prey, no questions asked.

Then she realised the hot, foul breath had faded, the grip on her leg gone. Felicity opened her eyes and found she was no longer halfway up a tree in the Whispering Woods but was, instead, in some sort of circular room with, she was relieved to see, Bob and Sophie. They looked as baffled and grateful as she felt.

'Now then, my dear,' said a voice. 'Rescue complete. Next step: payment.'

Chapter Eight
Pod

The creature before them was definitely what Felicity would class as unusual, even for a fairy.

Its head seemed to be a dark green leaf which tapered to a point at the top, the little stem sprouting feathery red fronds which draped around his face like hair. He had a sharp, upturned nose, large pointed ears and pale green bushy brows.

His body looked like a bit of bark from the trees, with twiggy arms folded across it as the creature watched the three friends observe their rescuer.

Orange, birdlike legs ended in hooked talons, and leafy wings grew from his back. He looked neither welcoming nor hostile and Felicity wasn't quite sure what to make of him.

'Thank you for saving us back there,' she said. 'I don't know what we would have done if you hadn't shown up when you did.'

'Manners and gratitude are *always* appreciated, my

dear girl,' said the fairy. 'Though a price must still be paid, of course.'

'Of course.'

'Let's see what you just narrowly avoided,' he went on, snapping his twiggy fingers. An image appeared on part of a rounded wall before them. Gobblers filled it. Felicity watched in horror as they tore into a poor animal in the woods, turning her head as they crunched bones and ripped flesh from the carcass.

'Eat anything, they will,' said the fairy. 'Animals, fairies, *humans*. Also, rotten scraps, mulch, fungi and all sorts of detritus. The Gobblers aren't fussy – they gobble anything and everything, even wood sprites like myself.'

'You're a wood sprite?' said Sophie, beaming. 'Thanks for the rescue. Love your house, by the way.' She smiled sweetly at him.

'It's a pod, actually. A flying, fully camouflage-able pod. Which is why you couldn't see me before.'

'That's brilliant!' said Sophie. 'So, you fly around the Whispering Woods in this little round pod and no one can see you? I'd love to do that!'

The wood sprite allowed a smile to creep through. 'Well, now you are doing just that. It serves me well enough.'

'So, you patrol the woods then, do you?' said Bob. 'It's a good job you were out and about today and happened to arrive just in the nick of time.' He raised an eyebrow.

'Yes, well, there's no point showing up until folk are absolutely desperate, otherwise they turn you away, thinking they can outwit the woods. Then, they perish and I get nothing.'

'Selfless little creature, aren't you?' muttered Bob.

The wood sprite's eyes narrowed and Felicity decided it was time to jump in. Bob should know better than anyone not to anger the fairy folk, but she agreed with her friend. The sprite could have helped them earlier and saved them a lot of panic. She knew there was no point asking his name, as fairies rarely gave them freely, believing there was much power in a name, so instead, she asked: 'What's the price then, for saving us? And for hopefully taking us out of these woods?'

'Hmm,' the wood sprite scratched his head. 'Double the favour, double the price.'

'Of course,' said Bob under his breath.

'A secret and a promise,' said the wood sprite. 'Payment. And I will drop you at another side of the Whispering Woods – if you tell me which you desire, for there are many.'

Felicity, Bob and Sophie glanced at each other.

'What exactly do you mean by a secret and a promise?' asked Felicity.

The wood sprite considered the question, then said, 'I

would like a secret from the Human Realm and a collective promise from you all.'

'Okay – just give us a few minutes to talk it over,' said Felicity, wondering what on earth they were going to say. She huddled together with Bob and Sophie as they tried to work out the best answers to give this strange creature. At last, Felicity turned to him. She decided she would think of him as Pod, as she preferred knowing names and he did live in a pod, so it seemed appropriate.

'A secret: Even though a lot of people have a lot of wonderful things in the Human Realm it's often those who have less – or who are much less bothered about owning things – who are happier. I mean, really, that in the Human Realm we secretly feel more content without our treasures, as you might call them, and that is a treasure in itself.'

'Interesting,' said Pod. 'That will do.'

Felicity breathed a sigh of relief. 'Our promise: We three promise to always think highly of our heroic rescuer – that is, *you* – and will never forget the day you saved us from the Gobblers.'

It was a simple promise, true as it was, but Felicity hoped it was enough. She didn't want Pod to think they were trying to trick him, but she also didn't want any of them to commit to doing something for him which could slow down their progress, or mean having to return to the

Whispering Woods. Fairies were proud creatures, however, so she hoped it was enough.

'I will accept that,' said Pod.

All three of them grinned.

'Now, where am I dropping you? I don't go beyond the borders of the Whispering Woods, mind.'

'We're headed to the Dark Forest,' said Bob, 'so as close to that as you can, or to whichever side of the woods that will lead us there.'

'The Dark Forest, you say? Interesting.' Pod eyed them curiously, a sly look on his face. 'Haven't been there before then?'

'No,' said Sophie. 'Can't *wait* to see it though!'

'Hmm. Not many venture there. It can be what you might call *inhospitable*. Though I've never visited it myself, so I suppose *you* might find otherwise.'

'What's so inhospitable about it?' asked Felicity. It really must be an unpleasant sort of a place if even a fairy who lived in the Whispering Woods thought it so.

'The tr— I mean, someone said it was "hidden and deep" and, well, swirly? It sounds silly, I know, but I wondered if you knew what they meant by that?'

'I have thoughts on the matter but I'm not sure I should be giving out important information without further payment,' said Pod.

Bob rolled his eyes.

'Where we come from in the Human Realm we have free speech,' piped up Sophie. 'We don't have to trade information – we just say it freely.' Noting the glimmer of surprise on the wood sprite's face, she added, 'Surely that's another fact that allows us a few clues? Please?'

She smiled one of the most angelic smiles Felicity had ever seen her friend make and Felicity smothered a giggle. Fairyland was so unpredictable. One minute you were running from ravenous Gobblers up a talking tree and the next, you were in a flying pod with a leafy wood sprite watching your best friend try to bargain for information with sugary smiles. It seemed to be working though.

'I will tell you this,' said Pod cryptically. 'The Dark Forest requires certain *adaptations* from those who wish to travel there in comfort, and it is dark and wet and sprawling – full of ravines and mountainous terrain. To venture forth, you will need stamina! And that is all you will get from me on the subject.' He crossed his arms to emphasise the point.

'That helps us a bit. Thank you,' said Felicity, sensing that the wood sprite would give nothing more away. She wasn't quite sure if she wanted to hear more anyway. The Dark Forest sounded a bit bleak.

'Now, while we've been sharing all of this *free speech*,' Pod's eyes narrowed at them, 'my pod has been whizzing through the Whispering Woods with great haste, so I can now deposit you all at your destination and get back to what I'm supposed to be doing.'

Sophie opened her mouth to ask something else, then seemed to think the better of it and snapped it shut again.

'I will drop you at the edge of the Whispering Woods which will point you most favourably in the direction you seek and from there, you should follow the river until you find a water nymph and get what you need to enter the forest. Now – this feels about right. Time to disembark!'

Felicity chewed over what Pod had said as a trapdoor in the centre of his strange home opened up to reveal the ground below them. It may have whizzed through the Whispering Woods but daylight was rapidly fading, so they would need to find shelter soon, she realised.

Pod gave them each a very large leaf to sit upon, reassuring them that it was perfectly safe and they wouldn't fall off, before pushing them unceremoniously out of the trapdoor. They floated slowly to the ground and Felicity quite enjoyed the sensation.

The pod was hovering above them and in truth, it wasn't very high up so she suspected that if they *had* fallen off they would only have suffered a few minor bumps and bruises. They tucked the leaves behind a tree and waved goodbye to the already disappearing pod, which looked a bit like an oversize acorn.

The Whispering Woods lurked behind them while up

ahead, lay grassland populated with hedges, shrubs and scattered trees. Somewhere around here there must be a river, thought Felicity, and they needed to find it quickly – if possible, before night fell. She wondered how close they were now to the sea. She missed hearing the waves upon the shore and smelling the fresh tang of salt in the air.

'Well, *that* was interesting!' Sophie brought her back to the present. 'What a weird wee creature. At least he helped us though, even if he *did* have an odd method of payment. Those Gobblers were – well, I suppose, *disgusting*? Ferocious? Only *you* seem to have seen them properly Felicity. I wonder why.'

'Perhaps your abilities are beginning to make themselves known,' said Bob. 'You seem to sense the true nature of things and tap into that somehow. Secrets are revealed to you. You cracked the secret of the Causeway stones before, don't forget, and solved the riddles too.'

'I'm not sure I want to hear those trees whispering ever again.' Felicity shivered. 'They were creepy and not exactly friendly. Anyway, let's worry about my abilities – if I really do have any – later, and see if we can find this river.'

Suddenly, she didn't feel quite so keen about exploring the possibility of having magical powers. Their recent experiences had somewhat dampened her enthusiasm for magic again, and besides, there were more important things they needed to focus on.

The trio set off and before long, heard a river flowing off to their left.

'Found it!' said Sophie as the water came into view shortly afterwards. 'Now – how exactly does a person go about locating a water nymph?'

Chapter Nine
Nymph Magic

By the time Felicity, Bob and Sophie had made it to the riverbank, they were tired and hungry and not particularly in the mood for hunting water nymphs.

'Will we have to get in the water to find them?' asked Sophie.

'No, best not,' said Bob. 'They're tricksy, water nymphs. Better not to confront them in their natural habitat like that unless you want to be dragged underwater - which isn't ideal if you don't have gills! If they're about then we should be perfectly capable of spotting them from land.'

They decided to eat first, sharing a chicken pie stuffed with vegetables and gooey gravy, wrapped up in flaky pastry that melted on their tongue like snow. Dessert was a mug of hot chocolate each, with buttery shortbread shaped like stars and dusted with glittering sugar.

'Hmm, delicious,' sighed Sophie. 'I needed that. I also really need that magic crockery Felicity. It's brilliant!'

Felicity tidied everything away in her bag, smiling. 'Yes, it's pretty handy, isn't it? Though I'm afraid it doesn't seem to work at home in the Human Realm. I've tried it already.'

Sophie's face fell. 'Oh well, I'll just have to enjoy it as much as I can while I'm here then!' she said.

With darkness draping around them, Bob suggested they bed down for the night.

'We might be in a hurry but we're no use to anyone tired,' he said, 'and it's getting darker earlier now, with all this unrest in the realm. Things are afoot at night that are best avoided.'

Felicity agreed they were tired, but she was itching to get on with their journey. Why waste another night when they could look for the water nymph now? The realm was always dangerous in her opinion and she thought that perhaps Bob was being overly cautious. She felt refreshed now they'd eaten and rested a little.

'I think I'm going to have a quick look around for this nymph first,' she said. 'I know we're all tired but I feel I have enough energy left to do that at least. I promise I won't go far – and I'll come back straightaway if I find anything - or anyone. There might be somewhere more sheltered further along the bank too, where we can rest.'

'I'm coming too,' said Sophie at once, jumping up and flashing a white-toothed grin. 'I'm not going to miss seeing a water nymph!'

'Let's all go together then,' said Bob. 'You're right Felicity – we might find shelter as we go along the bank, and it's best if we stick together. A quick look can't hurt.'

Felicity smiled gratefully at the brownie as they gathered their few belongings and set off along the riverbank. It was darker than it should have been for the time of year, but dusky light still lingered enough to see by as they journeyed on, their eyes scouring the water for any signs of activity.

When the river wound down through a tangle of trees to a small cove, they stopped. To follow it on land they would have to retrace their steps, but just as Felicity turned to go, she noticed a rowing boat tucked under a cluster of bushes near the water's edge.

'Perhaps the best way to find a water nymph is to be *on* the water, not beside it,' she said, eyes gleaming. 'If we can't go *into* the river then I'd say this is the next best thing, wouldn't you? And we're less likely to run into anyone else if we're out there on the boat.'

'It's dark and getting darker, though,' said Sophie. 'What if there's a waterfall – or rapids? We won't see danger until it's too late.'

'I thought that Bob could maybe conjure us up a light? Like you did once before, with the seaweed lantern?'

'I can certainly create a *little* light,' said the brownie, 'and the moon will soon be rising, so that will help.' He looked at the boat doubtfully. 'That thing might have holes in it, for all we know. It looks like it's been here a while, but I suppose it's worth a try.'

Once they'd turned the boat over, however, Felicity saw with relief that its base was fully intact, with no obvious signs of damage. It could have done with a fresh coat of paint, but otherwise, seemed perfectly capable of doing its job.

They hauled the vessel, which had three panels of wood stretched across the inside for seats, down to the water, Felicity the last to jump in as she pushed them away from the bank. They'd found oars stowed away inside it, so Bob and Sophie started rowing first, while Felicity peered into the water in the hope of spotting a nymph.

The night was quiet and cool, the water licking the sides of the boat soothing. They took turns to row and the moon rose above them, shining a silver path upon the river. Somewhere below them, music began to play, dark shapes gliding through the water as singing bubbled up to the surface.

The water nymphs had arrived.

***

It became quickly apparent that the nymphs did not want Felicity, Bob, Sophie, or their recently acquired craft on the river. The water grew increasingly choppy around them as the creatures gathered, swimming furiously beneath the boat and on all sides of it so that it rocked dangerously, caught in the churn of activity. They were like flies trapped in a watery web controlled by too many angry nymphs to count.

'What now?' gasped Sophie.

'Just hold tight,' said Felicity. 'The main thing is that we've found them. I'm going to try talking to one of them.'

She dipped her hand into the seething river before anyone could stop her, gripping the side of the boat with her other one. 'We're trying to reach the Dark Forest,' she called. 'We were told to find a water nymph to get what we need to enter it. Please, can you help?'

The boat rocked even more violently in response, tipping up on one side until Felicity felt sure they would all tumble into the water and be drowned by the creatures. What happened instead, however, was that the boat fell with a slap back onto the river and a head broke through the surface.

Felicity watched in silence with Bob and Sophie as water sluiced off the nymph's skull, long grey hair plastered to the sides of the sharp-featured face that emerged before them, the rest fanning out around her head. She had a slim white neck with gills. Nothing else of the nymph's body was revealed, as the rest of her stayed submerged. Her eyes were large and pale and violet, her gaze hostile but curious. When she spoke, her voice gurgled as if she was speaking underwater.

'Why should I help you? Especially when you are trespassing on our river and spoiling our moonlight parade. We owe you no favours and are not in the habit of granting them besides.' Her eyes narrowed.

'We apologise for trespassing and interrupting your evening,' said Felicity, Sophie nodding enthusiastically beside her, 'and I wouldn't ask if it wasn't *really* important, but we *have* to reach the Dark Forest for the sake of the realm.' She wasn't sure how much information she should share about that, but the nymph's eyes had brightened.

'The moon is waning,' she murmured, in that gentle bubbling voice. 'She is being drained of her light nightly and it is affecting us all. It is disrupting the ebb and flow of the tides and upsetting the natural balance of things. Are you going to fix the moon?'

'I … well … I certainly hope so, yes,' said Felicity. 'We're trying to sort everything out in the realm and that means the moon too. We just need to —'

'Reach the Dark Forest,' interrupted the nymph. 'Come here, child. If you are lying, I will drag you and your companions down to the riverbed, but if not, then I shall help.'

Felicity gulped as she leaned across to the nymph, who slowly raised dripping arms from the water. She placed one cold webbed hand on either side of Felicity's neck, murmuring as she did so, then brushed a thumb over Felicity's mouth, telling her to close her eyes. She placed her thumbs on Felicity's eyes also, and Felicity felt coldness at each spot on her body where the nymph had been, followed by tingling. The nymph did likewise to Sophie and Bob. Sophie looked baffled by it all, but said nothing.

'The magic worked, which tells me you are true of heart,' said the nymph. 'This boat will now take you to the gateway of the Dark Forest. It will run on magic and will not alter its course until you reach your destination. You will know it when you see it – and when the boat stops. You must go through the water-wall and enter the Monster Whirl.

'My gifts will ensure you safe passage in the forest – you will see and breathe as normal and will be able to navigate deep into it without succumbing to pressure which would otherwise snap your bones and pulverise your soft flesh and brains. Save the moon for us and we will be forever in your debt.'

The nymph disappeared back under the water as the three friends tried to take in all that she had told them worry, fear, excitement and sheer confusion flickering across their faces. Before they could speak a word to one another, the boat rose up above the river, buoyant on nymphs, who then pushed it forward with all their might so it skimmed along the water like a stone. Felicity gulped for breath and gripped the side of the vessel, Bob and Sophie doing likewise.

The boat kept up its fantastical pace for the rest of the night, but travelled so smoothly that Felicity, Bob and Sophie were rocked to sleep as one-by-one, they lay down and succumbed to their tiredness. Above them, the moon looked palely on.

**

The stillness woke them, as the moon bade her farewell and morning arrived, clean and clear as glass. The boat had stopped.

Felicity's mouth dropped open when she saw they had left the river and were now bobbing on the open ocean. She turned at Sophie's gasp, and swallowed. Before them rose a huge wall of water which reached impossibly high into the sky, and yet, there it was.

'The water-wall,' she breathed. 'And we have to go through it.'

'It's beautiful,' said Sophie. 'Freaky, but beautiful. Like a big pane of glass stretched across the sea. I think I can manage the water-wall, but I'm not so sure about the – what was it called? A *Monster* Whirl?'

'Yes, I think we might deduce by now what *that* will be,' said Bob, grimacing.

'We can?' Sophie raised her eyebrows at him. 'I have a feeling it will surprise *me,* anyway.'

Felicity stared at her friend and then felt her own neck. Gills. Just like Sophie – and Bob, she now noticed – she had grown gills since meeting the nymph.

'Ah,' Sophie saw what she was doing and checked her neck too. 'I sure hope these disappear when we get back home. *Not* very flattering, I think!'

They had a quick breakfast of strong, milky tea and buttery toast from Felicity's crockery, then readied themselves for crossing the water-wall.

'Okay – here goes,' said Felicity, picking up an oar and rowing with Bob. 'Time to face the Monster Whirl.'

Chapter Ten
Monster Whirl

The little rowing boat slipped through the water-wall as smoothly as a fish. Felicity's heart sank, however, when she saw what lay before them. This side of the water-wall was everything the other was not.

Here, choppy little waves jumped around them like hungry piranhas, splashing icy foam onto their skin. Sharp gusts of wind helped to churn up the sea, howling in their ears like a banshee and tugging at Felicity and Sophie's hair like a schoolyard bully. The sky was bruised purple, the sea a dark and uninviting beast that seemed to be sucking them into its lair, for the boat was moving against the snapping waves without the aid of oars, and they were all three of them powerless to stop it.

'What now?' yelled Sophie above the noisy gusts, her cheeks white as chalk.

'Just hold on and hope for the best!' Felicity called back. 'Bob?'

The brownie, who was gripping the side of the boat and looking rather green about his gills, managed to give a weary thumbs-up. Hold on it would have to be, thought Felicity grimly. But something made her trust the nymph, who so desperately wanted them to save the moon, and that helped to calm her a little, despite everything that loomed around them.

The boat was picking up its pace now, the wind shrieking even more loudly around them. Felicity spied at last what must be the Monster Whirl. She gulped.

Instead of slapping at the boat, the vicious little waves ahead were now moving in an anticlockwise direction, swirling past them giddily like frothy dancers caught up in a wild jig they couldn't escape from.

They curved away into the distance and Felicity wondered just how far they went before they swirled full-circle. By now, she knew for certain what they were to face and, as the boat reached the cusp of it, she gasped at the gigantic whirlpool they teetered over. It truly *was* a Monster Whirl.

Having reeled them in to its periphery, the magical Monster Whirl, which seemed possessed with its very own sly personality, appeared to take pleasure in the three friends' fear.

Bob, Sophie and Felicity clutched the boat with white-knuckled hands, shivering from the wet and the cold of the icy water which splashed them, and from sheer terror at what they guessed was about to happen.

Felicity felt sure they should have fallen into this watery monster's lair by now, and yet here they sat, dangling like hooked fish above the yawning cavern below. She couldn't see the bottom.

Water whirled fiercely around them - too loudly to even entertain the thought of shouting encouragement, or anything else, to one another - funnelling deep down into the ocean, the walls of water seeming to narrow on the descent. Wind filled this vortex and Felicity felt sure that at any moment they would be flicked down into that void and tumble fathoms below.

However, the boat finally began to move again, as if the Monster Whirl had decided they had seen enough, and they moved with the waves, around and around and around and around and around and around and around and around, until Felicity felt dizzy and seasick and had to close her eyes as the monster whirlpool danced them around its large outer rim, drawing them bit by bit into the heart of the ocean itself.

As they descended, the boat spun faster and faster, Sophie's screams mixing with the wails of the wind, until her voice gave out to hoarseness and she was forced silent. The speed of travel and the relentless wind made it difficult to breathe and Felicity found herself gulping air, trying to drink it into her body. But they had each grown gills and she knew that soon, air wouldn't matter. It would become the enemy and water the oxygen they required.

She hoped it would be as easy as when she had transformed into a mermaid the last time she swam underwater in the Fairy Realm. It had felt strange, but she'd been pleasantly surprised at how easy it had been, and how quickly she'd adapted to it all. Would they grow tails this time, she wondered?

Faster and faster they spun – and then, Sophie was flung right out of the boat. Felicity, who had been opening her eyes now and again despite her queasiness, could only watch in horror as her friend was siphoned off into the watery wrinkles of the Monster Whirl. She tried yelling to Bob, but he was whisked away next, and then Felicity found her own tired fingers forcibly pried away from the boat, and she gave in and let herself be sucked into the whirlpool.

Water flooded her vision and gurgled in her ears and around her, everything went black.

***

Felicity opened her eyes and swallowed a scream.

It was sheer exhaustion which prevented her from

vocalising her fear as she found herself staring into the inquisitive eyes of a rather humungous blubbery creature. She thought its head was easily the size of about five of her own. It had eyes of liquid black, a drooping whiskered snout and plump silky-looking cheeks that she imagined were cushiony-soft. Folds of skin piled around its neck like a coiled spring and its body seemed to extend an awfully long way behind it. It was a mountain of flesh and yet, it had so far failed to eat her and she rather thought, upon closer inspection, that its slow-blinking eyes were actually quite kindly-looking.

They were in a pocket of air within, she guessed, the Monster Whirl and thankfully, Bob and Sophie were there too.

Sophie's mouth formed a silent 'oh'. 'Where *are* we?' she breathed. Her friend's brow furrowed. 'We don't get elephant seals on the north coast of Northern Ireland. Well, not that I know of, anyway!'

The giant seal turned its head to her. Its voice was low and rumbly and sounded as if it was eating gravel. 'But this is Fairyland, surely you are aware of that? And the geography of the Fairy Realm and the distribution of its inhabitants is so very much different from the Human Realm. Here, you will find all sorts of creatures in all sorts of places – in the expected and the unexpected.

'We live under different laws here and magic makes a

muddle out of everything, you know.' He – for it sounded like a male, Felicity thought – paused. 'And I prefer *beachmaster,* if you please. Speaking of which, I need to be getting back to my dear old beach – don't want any turf wars breaking out. I'm merely here to supervise your entry to Ghost Reef, which,' he said to Sophie, 'exists a good bit further down, no doubt, than the reefs in the Human Realm, but it is a reef nonetheless and one in which I am tasked to deposit *you.* Take your final breaths, travellers, because from hereon in, it's water all the way.'

Felicity found her voice at the same time as Bob.

'What do you – ?'

'Why are – ?'

'Go ahead,' said Bob.

'What do you mean, you're here to see us to Ghost Reef? How did you know we were coming and what, exactly, *is* Ghost Reef?'

'Water speaks, I listen,' said the seal solemnly. 'And it's such a rarity to have travellers coming through that I felt compelled to see you on your way. Save the moon, save the realm – we all want to see what you can do … though not *all* of us, of course. Beware the beasts who wish you ill.

'Now, I see your gills have all come through, so off with you. Ghost Reef will explain itself when you see it. You're ocean-dwellers now for the foreseeable and should

88

feel quite at home. Remove your shoes and then, begone!'

Felicity saw that her hands had become webbed somewhere along the way and she guessed it must be the same with her and the others' feet too. She was glad she wasn't wearing her best shoes as she pulled her trainers off along with her socks. She went to remove her cloak as well, as she thought it would be cumbersome to swim in, but the elephant seal shook his head.

'The rest of your clothing will adapt. You will see.'

He surveyed them with satisfaction, and then, before Felicity had time to ask anything else of him, he swung his hind flippers towards her and batted her back into the Monster Whirl's heaving mass. Water filled her nostrils like air and she found she could breathe comfortably, which lessened her panic.

Felicity let the water carry her onwards, and soon, a cluster of white spectres appeared up ahead. The frenzied water had finally calmed and she swam towards the bleached coral that was Ghost Reef.

Chapter Eleven
At Ghost Reef

Felicity waited at Ghost Reef until her friends floated into view, grinning with relief from her perch on a piece of twisted coral.

She saw their clothes now had the appearance of fish scales like her own, which must be the final transformation so they could survive underwater. Felicity's cloak had also changed into a long, tapering fin, which she found she could raise and lower at will. She hoped it might help propel her more quickly through the water, if needs must.

'Well now!' said Bob, when he saw her. 'How is it that when I'm with you Felicity, I discover parts of Fairyland I never have before?' He grinned at her. 'This is something else altogether.'

The brownie's voice sounded a bit bubbly and distorted but was otherwise the same. Being underwater made Felicity feel freshly energised, though the burden of the task at hand still weighed heavily upon her.

'So – the Rhyming Riddler lives at the bottom of the ocean?' She shook her head. 'No wonder he can never be found! Who on earth would ever think of looking for him down here?'

'Yes, it explains why he so easily disappears,' said Bob. 'The Mountain of Lore must be one of the ancient oceanic ridges, which few know of and even fewer have seen. I only know vaguely of them because of my books, though marine ecology isn't a subject I've read much about.'

'Soph?' Felicity turned to her other friend.

'I watched a programme about "The Deep" once.' She frowned. 'But I can't really remember a lot about it, other than what Bob said. I mean, I don't think anyone back home has even explored *our* version of it very much. It can be rocky and mountainous, though, so that's probably where the Mountain of Lore comes in.'

'You can bet it's going to be a tricky place if the Riddler has it as his home,' said Felicity. 'Anyway, I suppose that, no matter what you expect to find in the Fairy Realm, it usually manages to surprise you. We'll just have to take things as they come.'

'It *is* ghostly though, isn't it?' said Sophie.

It was true, Ghost Reef was very well named, for it covered the seabed around them like a decaying skeleton.

Where there should have been a flurry of life amongst colourful coral, instead, scrawny fish drifted aimlessly through the bleached branches of the natural structure, giving an eerie and melancholy feel to the place.

A blot appeared in the distance and the three watched as a lone dolphin approached. Assuming it could speak, like most of the creatures in the realm, Felicity waited until it had swum up to them before she bid it hello and asked after its pod.

The creature shook itself, immediately transforming into a fishtailed fairy with webbed hands, two long scaly wings – or fins, Felicity supposed - upon its back. Male or female, she couldn't decide.

'Shapeshifter,' said Bob. 'Be gone! We need no "assistance" from you.'

The fairy hissed, baring spiky grey teeth at the brownie, but it turned to leave and swam off in what Felicity actually thought was more of a huff than a rage.

'Was that a *mermaid*?' said Sophie, eyes wide. 'Shouldn't we have asked it about the Mountain of Lore?'

'It wasn't a mermaid,' said Bob grimly. 'Shapeshifters can assume almost any form and are notoriously devious. The more you engage with them the more likely you are to fall under their thrall, which is why I dismissed that one so abruptly.'

'So, we had a lucky escape then,' said Sophie. She shivered. 'Still, a *shape*shifter!'

'Bob – do you still have the map?' asked Felicity.

'I do.'

They spread the map, which seemed to be waterproof, onto the coral, and at once, Felicity saw it had changed. Now that they were in the domain of the Dark Forest, it had become a very rough map of below sea level. She pointed at Ghost Reef in dismay.

'It's right at the top! And I thought we'd already gone so deep. Look, the Mountain of Lore is way down *there*.' She prodded the bottom of the map. Between them and the Riddler lay far too many levels for her liking.

'Ghost Reef, the Blue Forests, Twilight Zone, Midnight Zone, the Abysmal Realm, Challenger Deep,' recited Sophie. 'We have to get through all of *those*?'

'It would seem so,' said Bob, pressing his lips together grimly. 'It would appear that there is a whole other aquatic kingdom down here – and we're about to get acquainted with it!'

***

As Ghost Reef appeared to be nothing more than a wasteland, Felicity, Bob and Sophie decided to stay for a little while to practise their underwater swimming - now they had webbed feet and hands to contend with - and to acclimatise. Everything had happened so quickly and they agreed they would progress much faster when they set off again if they took some time to prepare.

Felicity was glad to see that they all took to the water quite naturally – even Bob – who declared himself very much a land-lover, but was fully open to embracing the present situation if it meant saving his friend, helping the realm and exploring a whole new underwater world.

Eating proved a little tricky, as they had to hold tight to their crockery to stop everything floating away, but oddly, it was otherwise quite manageable.

'It ought to be a lot darker down here than it is,' said Sophie, as they got ready to go. 'I suppose the nymph must have done something to our eyes to help us see better but it's bound to get even darker the deeper we go. We didn't tell her that we were going to the Mountain of Lore, so it might be *too* dark down wherever it is! It'll be hard keeping time too – knowing when it's day or night.'

Felicity frowned. 'Yes, I think you might be right, but we'll just have to take things as they come. And I vote we go on as much as we can until we feel tired. Rest when we need to but just keep swimming, no matter what time it is. We don't know how much time Fairyland has left, but it can't be much.'

'Good idea,' said Bob. 'Now – shall we strike out for the Blue Forests, whatever they might be?'

'Wow,' said Sophie, interrupting. 'Look!' She pointed behind Felicity and Bob, who were sitting opposite her on the reef.

Felicity's mouth dropped open, unintentionally mirroring the procession of creatures gliding noiselessly towards them. They had huge gaping mouths and Felicity could see right inside their bodies, where white bony structures – which she guessed were ribs - criss-crossed. They seemed to fly through the water, large fins spread out on either side, giving them a graceful appearance, though their open mouths made it look as if they were locked in a silent scream. They almost looked like flying saucers, and were approaching rapidly.

'It's okay, they're mantas. Manta rays, I mean,' said Sophie. 'They only eat plankton, so we're quite safe. They don't look right, though. They should be black on top and white underneath, not all ghostly white like these ones.'

'Ghost mantas for a Ghost Reef,' said Bob. He shivered.

The giant manta rays swooped up and over their heads, performing a graceful underwater ballet as they looped and swirled around them, before disappearing as silently as they had arrived.

'Beautiful.' Felicity looked at her friends. 'Well, we'd better be off, before any less friendly ghosts appear. This place is a bit eerie and it's sad to see a lovely coral looking more like a graveyard. Come on – let's go.'

They had a long way to travel if they were to find the Mountain of Lore and Felicity was eager to get moving. She knew they would surely face danger in the ocean, but it had dawned on her that the witches likely wouldn't follow them down here, and she felt sure they had dodged the spies too, as she hadn't felt that prickly sensation of being watched for a while. She felt freer down here, freshly rejuvenated and ready to tackle their challenge with gusto.

She thought it best if they swam fairly close to the seabed, as they could easily get disoriented in the vast blue deep, and it might help as a sort of landmark. She knew the water level above them would get higher the further out they went, but surely it would be easier to find shelter, and eventually, the Riddler's mountain, if they kept the seafloor in sight.

Leaving Ghost Reef behind, the three kicked off into the water with renewed vigour. It helped a little knowing something of what lay ahead, though Felicity was as unnerved as Sophie about having to navigate so many levels of the ocean to reach the Riddler's lair. At this stage, it was a bit late to be questioning the Enchanter's message, however. She just hoped her grandfather was correct, and that they would find whatever they needed to bring Butterkin and the rest of the missing fairy folk back from wherever they had been spirited away to by the enchanted pebbles.

The Enchanter had said this mysterious object would tell them where everyone was, but would it also play a part in physically retrieving them, Felicity wondered? She hoped so. Surely they couldn't be expected to travel to every single magical location to seek them out? They would be wandering forever, if so!

She shook the thought from her head as they swam through a shoal of fish. Sophie probably knew what species they were, Felicity mused. The creatures parted to let them pass, but she was sure they were muttering as they did so.

'Excuse me, we shouldn't have just swum through you,' she said. 'Sorry to disturb you.'

The fish eyeballed her, but continued with their mutterings. They were small and grey, with a black stripe running from their eyes to their tails.

'S'okay,' gasped one little fish, swimming up from the seabed towards her. 'They're not angry at you – they're just jittery because of *him*.'

Felicity didn't like the sound of that. 'Who?'

'We've just been mobbing him,' said the fish. Felicity looked back at him, puzzled and a little concerned. Mobbing? 'You *know* – squirting water at him so he can't hide and snatch fish away,' explained the little fish. 'Come and see. It's fun!'

'That's okay, we have somewhere to be,' said Felicity just as Sophie darted down to follow the fish. She should have known her nature-obsessed friend would want to see what was happening. Sighing, Felicity beckoned to Bob and they swam after Sophie, but found her alone and looking confused moments later.

'Where did all the fish go?' said Bob, looking annoyed.

'I don't know, but I don't like this,' said Felicity. 'Come on, let's go. We shouldn't be getting distracted anyway,' she added, looking pointedly at Sophie.

As she turned to leave, however, something in the sand caught her eye. She was sure it had moved – as if something was lurking underneath it. She remembered the little fish and its talk of 'mobbing'. Perhaps they'd stopped because someone had forced them to. By *eating* them. She whirled round just as the sand seemed to fall in on itself, revealing rows of sharp glistening teeth.

'*Sophie!*' she screamed. 'Watch out!'

Chapter Twelve
Watch Out, Bobbit About

Sophie yelled as two incredibly sharp rows of teeth crashed together within a seaweed's breadth of her foot. The water churned as she propelled herself towards Bob and Felicity, who reached for her arms and pulled her farther along.

'What *was* that?' she panted.

'Looks like some kind of giant – and very ugly – worm,' said Bob, gazing below them.

'Bobbit.'

The fish had returned, though there was no sign of the little one who had wanted to show off to them before.

'A *what*?'

'A Bobbit, but it's much too big,' said a fish slightly larger than the rest. 'It must have swallowed our mobbing team whole.' He looked mournful but then his face cleared. 'Well, we're out of here, and so should you be if you have any sense.'

The shoal turned as one and moved swiftly away.

'Look out,' said Sophie. 'It's coming back!'

The Bobbit, which Felicity now saw really *was* nothing more than a very large worm with a hideously vicious mouth, had shaken its entire head and part of its body from the sand. It rose up like a snake from a charmer's basket, bobbing its head, which opened at the top into those huge jagged jaws, revealing a gaping mouth from which protruded two antennae.

'It's looking for us,' whispered Sophie. 'Worms are blind so it must be trying to sense our movements.'

They stayed as still as they could, but it seemed the Bobbit had already gathered all the information it needed, as it suddenly reared up and scrabbled to get out of its hole.

'Enough of this. Let's get out of here,' said Bob, and they kicked off into the water while the Bobbit struggled to get free.

As Felicity risked a glance behind, she saw with horror that the vile creature had managed to get loose and was wriggling across the sand. The question was, would it swim up to them?

'Bobbit on the loose! Bobbit on the loose!' A flurry of fish fled past them, trailing bubbles. 'How? Most odd! Never seen before! Who's to blame?'

Felicity, Bob and Sophie swam as fast as they could, but the Bobbit was keeping pace below. What was it up to if it couldn't – or wouldn't - swim up to catch them, Felicity wondered? Perhaps it was trying to tire them out, hoping they would drop with fatigue into its waiting jaws? Well, Felicity was determined *that* wasn't going to happen. She *was* starting to feel weary, however. She stopped swimming.

'What do you want, Bobbit?' she called down.

The Bobbit stopped too and raised its head in the direction of her voice. Could a Bobbit speak? Or, more to the point, could a bigger than normal Bobbit acting as it normally wouldn't be able to speak in Fairyland? Felicity suspected so.

'What are you *doing*?' hissed Sophie.

'Don't worry. It doesn't seem to be able to leave the seafloor. I don't think it can swim up here.'

'You hope.' Sophie grimaced.

The Bobbit writhed slowly, stretching out its fat, glutinous body so they could see how long it was, tiny setae protruding from each segment like little teeth, though Felicity knew they were actually feet. In Fairyland, however, the animals might not have quite the same characteristics as back home, so she didn't want to assume anything about this nasty Bobbit creature.

She watched as it drew each segment towards its head, coiling up on itself almost like a —

'*Spring!*' yelled Felicity. 'He's going to spring himself up on us. Move – *now!*'

Just as she pushed Sophie out of the way, the Bobbit winched the last part of its body in, and then, like a cork from a bottle, launched itself from the seabed, flying towards them at breakneck speed. His jaws were open wide, waiting to crunch on flesh and bones. Remembering her cloak-turned-fin just in time, Felicity raised it quickly, moving out of the Bobbit's line of fire just as it whizzed past her foot. She looked up in time to see the Bobbit in the jaws of a large fish which seemed quite capable of disarming the creature.

'Well – now we know all about Bobbits, don't we?' said Sophie, breaking the tension. 'Didn't realise I'd be brushing up on my nature studies in Fairyland, Felicity, but hey, I'm all for it! Who doesn't enjoy a good old sea safari?'

Felicity smiled weakly at her friend. Bob just looked at Sophie as if she was mad.

'Come on,' said Felicity. 'Let's go.'

***

It wasn't long before the seascape around them changed again, sunlight dappling now through the water as swathes of seaweed overhead blocked out its rays. They seemed, somehow, to tire less in the water and had been moving steadily throughout the day though it was

102

difficult to tell just what time it was. The seaweed was a good sign, however, as Felicity was certain it meant they had reached the Blue Forests – or the beginning of them anyway.

'This is amazing,' said Sophie, as they swam under thick belts of bronzed kelp, thin silver fish darting amongst the fronds. 'I mean, I've been snorkelling before, but this is something else. I wish I had my underwater camera.'

Bob looked at her quizzically and she added hastily, 'Of course, we wouldn't have time for photography anyway, what with being on a magical mission and all …'

'Indeed.' The brownie smothered a smile.

'Do you think we should find someone to ask about the Riddler's lair?' said Felicity. 'I mean, we know roughly where we have to go, but the ocean is vast. What if we get lost? It would be easily done. I don't want to get stuck down here – gills or no gills. I'm worried about my family too. This is going to take us ages, by the looks of it.'

'Yes, I've been thinking about that,' said Bob. 'We don't want to alert the Riddler that we're coming, but we do need more direct directions, so I rather think we must. We'll just have to be careful about what we say and who we ask.'

It felt strange swimming through the sea with a forest of fronds above them, long, pole-like 'trunks' hanging down into the water. A group of grumpy-looking black fish with downturned mouths and empty eyes floated past, but Felicity didn't really feel like asking them for help. Anyway, they ignored the three travellers and had soon disappeared into the aquatic forest.

'I suppose they're called the Blue Forests because they're growing in "the Big Blue",' chattered Sophie. 'Because they're far from blue, aren't they, these seaweedy forests?' She stared around her, clearly delighted with her surroundings. Felicity nearly jumped out of her scales, however, when her friend gave a yelp shortly afterwards and darted to her side.

'There's something over there, watching,' she said. 'I saw an eye!'

Felicity stopped. Someone worth asking directions from, or someone who was likely to eat them? Her urgency for assistance won out over her fear of predators – for the moment – and she cautiously approached the rocky reef Sophie had fled from, hoping she wasn't about to make a huge mistake. It couldn't be a shark, she thought – it couldn't hide in such a small space, surely – and, off the top of her head, no other sea creatures came to mind that might be harmful. Of course, there was always the risk of it being an unfriendly underwater fairy, and her knowledge of sea creatures wasn't great.

The rocky outcrop rose up from the seabed like a

challenge. Felicity, Sophie and Bob had stayed further away from the bottom after their Bobbit experience, but as they'd moved deeper into the Blue Forests, Felicity had suggested they swim lower again, as there would be more chance of meeting other creatures down where there were nooks and crannies for living in and hiding from enemies.

Well, now it appeared they had found one such creature, so Felicity prepared herself to deal with this mysterious eye. All sorts of colourful seaweed grew over and around the rock where it lurked, including barnacles and various other shelled creatures.

The eye opened.

Felicity gasped, but stayed put despite her trembling. She fell back, however, when the owner of the eye began to dislodge itself from its resting place, her mouth dropping open in surprise.

From the very small crevice, sandwiched between the rocks, a long tentacle extended out towards her. It was pointed at the tip, growing thicker towards the body, and had a series of what looked like suckers on its underside. It waved around in the water for a few seconds as if checking for something, and then another appendage emerged – and another and another - until Felicity counted a total of eight.

The creature hefted itself out of its lair and she came face-to-face with a giant octopus. It rose up before her, all giant suckered arms and huge fleshy mass, its head bigger than all of theirs put together.

'Wow,' said Sophie, who had swum up beside Felicity.

Bob gaped and said nothing.

'Quick question,' said Sophie, before Felicity could speak. 'Are you going to eat us?'

The octopus stared at her and then surprised them all by laughing. It was so bizarre and unexpected that Felicity, Bob and Sophie started laughing too.

'No, I won't eat you, child,' said the octopus. 'I have a larder full of crabs and other delicacies and I've already eaten amply today.'

Sophie swallowed her laughter. 'Oh,' was all she said.

'Now, while this body has its uses and is very handy for squeezing into a tight spot, I think I'll just have a quick change,' said the octopus, raising its arms up over its body.

'It's turning inside-out!' said Bob in horror.

They watched as the octopus did just that, long fronds of seaweed spilling out from its centre, followed by a face, torso and more human-like arms. An incredibly long scaly tail finished the transformation.

'Are you a mermaid?' asked Felicity, not quite sure what to make of it all.

'I,' said the creature, 'am like nothing you've ever seen before. I am an octo-woman. Now – what can I do for you?'

Chapter Thirteen

Octo-woman

Felicity wasn't sure what to make of the mermaid-type creature in front of her with its seaweed hair, who just seconds ago had been a giant octopus. One thing she *was* sure of, though, was that the folk of the Fairy Realm rarely offered their help for free, and were prone to trickery. So, she hoped Sophie and Bob remembered not to give away the specifics of what they were doing. Who knew what creatures down here were on the Riddler's side – or the witches', for that matter? They would have to be careful.

Bob and Sophie appeared to be waiting for her to take the lead, so she said, 'We've been travelling for some time and just wanted to check if we're headed in the right direction. We haven't seen anyone in a while, so when Sophie spotted you, we thought we'd come over and ask for help. We're sorry if we've disturbed you.' Just how sorry would depend on what this octo-woman said – or did – next, she thought uneasily.

'It is most odd to be awoken by a party consisting of what appears to be a brownie and two human girls,' said the creature, large black eyes blinking slowly at Felicity. They were the sort of eyes you could get lost in, she imagined, if you stared into them for too long. 'What is your purpose and where do you wish to go? If I know *that,* then perhaps I can assist.'

This was the tricky bit. If the octo-woman wasn't an ally, then just how much could Felicity reveal without raising suspicion, when they were already drawing attention to themselves by their very presence? She decided to say as little as possible about their final destination and instead, asked for help to get to the next place on the map.

'We'd like to visit the Twilight Zone,' she said. 'My friend Sophie here is a marine biologist in training, so we wanted to explore a little. We're from the Human Realm, yes, but managed to find our way through to Fairyland and couldn't resist the expedition.'

She decided to stop talking, as she really wasn't sure if the octo-woman would buy her story. It sounded a bit unbelievable, even to Felicity. The octo-woman seemed concerned with only one thing, however.

'I hope this doesn't mean there will be more of you coming down here?!' she exclaimed. 'Humans in "The Deep"? Whatever next?'

'Is there nowhere sacred to us creatures anymore? Next thing you know they'll be flooding the place with their plasticky rubbish and catching us all for their supper. We animals of the sea speak to one another across borders, you know. It's much easier for us, as no one can see what goes on in "The Deep". And here in the Fairy Realm there's refuge for creatures from your realm too, who can adapt to living here no matter where they're from, thanks to our oceanic magic.

'But if humans invade then we're all doomed, for Fairyland is the final haven for aquatic creatures!'

She looked distraught and Felicity felt a bit more confident about trusting this strange creature because of it. 'Don't worry, it's just us,' she reassured her. 'We're actually trying to help make sure that *doesn't* happen.'

She realised, thanks to the octo-woman's outburst, that this was yet another potential threat to the kingdom which she hadn't considered. If Fairyland's borders were weakening and letting all manner of ghouls and monsters through from other magical realms, then the border between the human world and that of the fairies might also be loosening. It wouldn't do at all to have the realm overrun by curious humans, who would surely want to experiment on and examine any creature they found – above or below water.

Felicity knew her own world wasn't in the best state

these days, what with pollution and hunting and the general carelessness of people; she certainly didn't want Fairyland to go the same way. The folk here might have magic, but who knew what would happen if magic mixed with the technology and military power of her world? She shivered. The octo-woman was studying her with curiosity.

'So you *don't* want to explore? You lied to me?' she said, anger flaring in those eyes.

'Oh, we do want to explore the Twilight Zone – and elsewhere,' said Felicity quickly. 'We just aren't sure what we're looking for, or how exactly to get there. Back on land, things are getting a bit out of hand, with folk disappearing and darkness creeping into the realm, so we just acted on instinct – thought it might be better to look around down here, out of the way.'

She was starting to tire of this conversation. If the octo-woman couldn't help them, then they were just wasting time, and Felicity had run out of cover stories. The octo-woman seemed to believe her though.

'I suppose you seem harmless enough,' she said. 'And there's worse than me down here, so if you're not what you seem then someone else will no doubt sort you out.

'These are the Blue Forests, comprising a mixture of marine meadows, kelp gardens and saltwater trees. They can be confusing if you don't know the way through them and you are only on the outskirts, I'm afraid.

'My advice is to continue on as you were and see if you can catch yourself a sea otter. They're the guardians of the kelp forests and know the layout of the sea around here better than anyone. They tend to forage for urchins on the seafloor before sunrise, then again in the afternoon, so are generally done by sunset, though some forage at midnight too, so you might come across one if you keep going. It's approaching sunset now.'

'Don't otters need to get back to the surface quickly to breathe?' asked Sophie.

'So you know your creatures, do you, girl?' The octo-woman shook her head. 'As I said before, in the Fairy Realm, we function a little differently. A sea otter in your world may need to go back above water after a few minutes on the ocean floor, but here, it's a different story. Now you *think* you know them – now you *know* you do not. They aren't the most social animals either, but I'm sure if you find one it'll point you in the right direction. Now, if that's all, I'll be getting back to sleep.'

'Yes, I think we should be going,' said Felicity. 'Thanks for your help. We'll look out for an otter!'

The octo-woman bowed her head, the seaweed hair dancing around her as she curled in on herself to turn outside-in again. Felicity wasn't quite sure how it all worked, but one minute there was a sort-of woman in front of her and the next, a giant octopus waving huge suckered arms. Unbelievably, it managed to fold itself up onto the small ledge between the rocks once more, closing its eyes to sleep and putting an end to their conversation.

Bob, who had remained quiet throughout the whole exchange, breathed a sigh of relief. 'Things with eight legs give me the creeps,' he whispered. 'Especially when they come in giant form!'

The octopus opened an eye and Felicity kicked off into the water. Time to go.

***

In truth, the octo-woman hadn't been overly helpful in the end, as Felicity, Bob and Sophie kept swimming in the direction they had been and Felicity knew that if they'd come across a sea otter they'd likely have asked it for help anyway, whether they knew it was a guardian of the kelp forests or not.

They were swimming closer to the seabed now, on the look-out for foraging otters, and always keeping their eyes peeled for nasty Bobbits. It really was a marvel, thought Felicity, taking it all in with awe. The ocean was the ultimate illusionist, she thought, as it showed no sign of its colourful treasures to those above. No, to enjoy the wealth of wonderful creatures and plants living in the sea you had to dive down and discover those secrets for yourself.

Above them wafted a thick canopy of seaweed which would have blocked out the fading rays of the sun, but in fairy waters or, perhaps, with their new underwater fairy sight, they were still able to see where they were going, though it was darker now that day had nearly passed. Amongst the upper seaweed fronds floated wispy little shrimps which were almost invisible, while sea snails and crabs clung to the foliage. Beneath them, an assortment of fish went about their business and on the seafloor they saw everything from orangey sea stars and anemones, to the otters' favourite snack of sea urchin.

Rocks jutting up into the water looked almost as if someone had covered them with a bright patchwork quilt. Felicity couldn't identify half of what was growing, attached, or just wandering about upon them, but she was mesmerised by it all.

Here was a white mushroom-type plant with a fluffy head that looked like a cauliflower, there was a nest of spiny urchins – purple, blue and red. Dotted amongst these was mossy, emerald seaweed, along with mussels, clams and much more. It was bewitching, and Felicity felt honoured to be treated to such a spectacle that so few people ever saw.

They then moved into what she guessed was one of the marine meadows the octo-woman had mentioned, full of gently swaying seagrass and darting fish. At one point they saw a strange pre-historic-looking creature walking through the meadow, using its stumpy but wide trunk-like nose to hoover up the seagrass. It was the size of a small cow and was wandering along with its eyes closed.

The friends swam on.

'Maybe we should rest here for a while, where there's cover?' suggested Bob. 'I don't see any otters.'

Felicity was keen to keep going but also, admittedly, a little tired. They stopped in the meadow. It was getting gloomier with every stroke they swam. She saw something move out of the corner of her eye and whirled round, but it was only seaweed bobbing in the water. After a few minutes, however, she couldn't shake the feeling she was being watched, so she swam closer to have a look.

As she approached the weed, a shrill voice rang out.

'Keep your distance, or risk the wrath of the mighty sea dragon!'

Chapter Fourteen
Secrets and Sea Dragons

Felicity paused in front of the blubbery seaweed, a dense mass which, really, could be hiding anything. She wondered at the thin, reedy voice though. Could a mighty sea dragon really possess such a pitiful set of pipes?

Sophie and Bob joined her. 'Did somebody say something?' asked Sophie.

'Apparently, there's a mighty sea dragon somewhere in there,' said Felicity, pointing at the seaweed, 'but I'm not so sure.'

'Mighty?' Sophie scoffed. 'Don't be silly. Someone's having you on. Sea dragons are related to sea*horses*. They're tiny! I mean, I think they're maybe a bit bigger but they're still small – not like a land dragon and not something that's likely to eat us, anyway. Unless fairy sea dragons are very different from ours back home. Where is it? It'd be awesome to see one.'

Before Felicity could answer, the voice spoke again,

this time, sounding more than a little disgruntled. 'I'm not *small* – I'm perfectly proportioned according to my environment and I'm superbly camouflaged into the bargain!'

That part was true at least, for Felicity could see nothing but seaweed and grass. No sea dragons anywhere, except for the annoyed voice.

'We didn't mean to offend you,' she said, wishing they didn't have to keep apologising all the time. 'Will you come out so we can see you? Don't worry, we're harmless.'

'You wouldn't be able to catch me even if you were harm*ful*,' said the voice, and at last, the owner emerged.

In the gloom, Felicity could just see a marmalade-coloured creature with a long thin nose shaped like a trumpet and a body that resembled an orange segment. Its skin was speckled and it had a long neck with what looked like little leaves growing out from the sides of both it and the rest of its tiny body. It was these strange protrusions which made it closely resemble a floating piece of seaweed. Very clever camouflage indeed, Felicity agreed. It was an unusual-looking creature, but seemed harmless. When it spoke again, Felicity could see it had no teeth.

'What is your business here?' said the sea dragon suspiciously. 'You're a strange group to be seeing in these parts.'

'Yes, so people keep telling us,' said Sophie, grinning.

'We're on our way to the Twilight Zone,' said Bob. 'Any chance you could tell us if we're going the right way?'

'We were looking out for a sea otter, as we were told they know the lie of the, er, water, better than most, as guardians of the kelp forest, but we haven't managed to find any,' added Felicity.

The little leafy sea dragon puffed out its chest. 'I know a good bit about where things are too,' he said. 'But why are you going so far into "The Deep"? What's your business down here?'

Felicity decided to come part-way clean with the creature about their intentions, as she was tired of spinning stories and for whatever reason, she liked this sea dragon.

'To be honest, we're not sure who to trust down here, or what to tell folk we meet, because we're on a very important journey, which we need to get on with quickly, and can't afford to be delayed or, well, stopped. That's why we're going to the Twilight Zone – and beyond that still.'

The sea dragon had tiny eyes like beads, set into a nugget of a head. They lit up at Felicity's words.

'Well now, then I really *can* help you,' he said proudly. 'Not only do I know the geography of "The Deep", but I also have a pretty thorough knowledge of who's to be trusted, because I make it my business to know who lives and goes where. If I don't, I get eaten. I hide in the kelp and seagrass but learn from fish who drift into my habitat, and my cousins the seahorses keep me in the loop too. I may not travel far myself, but I'm a font of information.

'In fact, I'll tell you a secret, if you like. Well, it's not *such* a secret down here, but I think it's little known to land-dwellers.' He paused. 'Would you like to hear it?'

'Please, yes,' said Felicity.

The sea dragon looked at them conspiratorially. 'Well, down in "The Deep" – right near the bottom – lies a place full of all sorts of strange things from all sorts of strange places. Even *more* peculiar – a little magic man lives inside this place and talks in a very odd manner. That is to say – he rhymes! Now, what do you make of that?!'

***

The sea dragon's confirmation of the Rhyming Riddler's lair really being at the bottom of the ocean filled Felicity with relief. At least they were on the right track with their expedition. Thank goodness the Enchanter was as clever as he was. With her family still prisoners, only she and her friends could help to return the lost fairy folk and heal the borders, so it was important they didn't get lost. Even if they had escaped, she reasoned, the Enchanter, her mum and Granny Stone would still be needed to battle against the witches and goblins. She just hoped they could do what needed to be done, and in time, before the Fairy Realm was consumed by darkness.

'What else do you know about this magic man?' she asked.

'Not a lot, I'll admit,' said the sea dragon. 'He's rarely seen – he must have a quick way up to the surface from his mountain – but he's not very friendly, from what I hear, and he's a bit of a pilferer. Likes to steal things.'

'Hmm, we know,' said Felicity. 'We've run into him before, on land.'

'Not a friend of yours, I hope?'

'No, not at all!' She wondered if it might be worth the risk of asking how to find the Mountain of Lore. They really needed to hurry and didn't have the luxury of mistrusting every creature they met. Besides, the sea dragon didn't seem to be a fan of the Riddler either.

'We're trying to find him, actually,' she said. 'We think he has something which we need rather urgently. It's probably stolen and we have to get it back without him knowing. Do you know the best and quickest way to find him?'

The sea dragon studied them carefully, then seemed to make his mind up about something. 'Follow me into the kelp,' he said. 'Best to discuss this in more private quarters.'

They followed the sea dragon into the thick slippery kelp, where the creature almost disappeared, he was so well camouflaged. He stopped once they'd gone quite far into this particular patch, which was thankfully quite a large one.

'The way you mean is not one many dare, or indeed, *want* to take,' he said. 'However, it is possible to go to where you speak of, but it's a good job you bumped into me, as you'll need some reinforcements to venture that far down into "The Deep". To the Challenger Deep.' He shivered. 'The Twilight Zone has very little light, even fairy light, so you will need to have your eyes further adapted for that.' He looked them up and down.

'Probably best to reinforce your bodies too, for the extreme cold and the extra pressure. It gets *very* pressurised the further down you go, especially in the Abysmal Realm, which will lead you into the lair of the rhyming man. Are you sure about this?'

Felicity swallowed nervously. It sounded impossible to venture so far into the dangerous deep, but what other choice did they have?'

'We're sure,' she said in unison with Bob and Sophie. She smiled at her friends in thanks. They were all nervous about what lay ahead, but she knew she could rely on them.

'How do we get, er, reinforced?' she asked.

'Simple!' said the sea dragon. 'You hitch a ride with a Leatherback, who will have all you need to get fortified and, if you're *very* lucky, it might take you as far as the Midnight Zone, the final zone before the Abysmal Realm. After that, you're on your own.'

Felicity knew Leatherbacks were giant sea turtles – the largest type of turtle in fact. She'd seen pictures of them and learned a bit about the creatures when her class had visited their local coastal centre. She wasn't sure what the sea dragon meant about hitching a lift though, as they certainly weren't big enough to carry two girls and a brownie.

As if reading her mind, the sea dragon said, 'Of course, I mean, the Leatherback will guide you and help you along. They're sacred creatures, so you must not try to ride one like a whale.'

'Why don't we just find a big whale instead then?' asked Sophie.

'If you're in a hurry it will take too long to summon one from the Big Blue. And you'd have to go deep just to find one. Leatherback is a better bet. Besides, you need *fortified*.'

'Oh, yeah.'

'And we should trust you because …?' said Bob. 'This all sounds good, but we have to careful, as Felicity said. We have folk looking for us – not good ones.'

The sea dragon looked offended and stuck his long trumpet nose up at them. 'I happen to be very trustworthy, I'll have you know. I'm not a spy for anyone. What you need to be wary of are sly, deceitful worms like those awful Bobbits, as well as certain fish, octopuses and sharks, though not all. The sea witches are in league with the land witches too, so — '

'Sea witches?' Felicity had forgotten there were sea witches, but now she remembered the Riddler had mentioned one the last time she saw him. 'So they could be watching us – and have spies all over the place. We've already met a Bobbit – and an octo-woman. Was *she* a witch, do you think?'

'A cousin,' said the sea dragon. 'Who might or might not tell the witches she's seen you. It's hard to know.' He looked a bit nervous now. 'I don't want to be caught aiding and abetting, so how about I get you out of here, pronto?'

'Sounds good to me,' said Felicity. She felt disoriented, not knowing what time it was, or where in the ocean they were, though it was surely night-time by now.

The sea dragon disappeared deeper into the kelp, re-emerging shortly afterwards looking pleased with himself. 'I put out a call for the closest Leatherback. I think there might be one in the area right now, so you should be in luck.'

Felicity wondered how he had called the turtle as they

had heard nothing. Sophie must have read her mind, as she voiced the question.

'I used my horn, though you wouldn't be able to hear it, not being a Leatherback,' said the sea dragon, and Felicity realised he meant his nose. She hid a smile, as she didn't want to offend the little creature. Whatever next?

It wasn't very long before there was a stirring in the kelp, as if something was trying to get in, and the sea dragon went to have a look. He returned quickly, looking triumphant. 'My new friends! It's time to move on. Your Leatherback has arrived!'

They followed him out of the kelp and saw a large dark shape hovering in the gloomy water. It was so dark by now, though, that they couldn't see which end was front and which the back.

'Now, Leatherbacks usually stay in shallower waters at night and don't dive for longer than a few minutes at a time,' said the sea dragon. 'But I've explained your situation and our friend here is happy to make an exception to his usual routine, to assist you all. Time to get you fortified for the journey ahead!'

Chapter Fifteen
Into 'The Deep'

The fortification process didn't take very long, but was quite unusual. Along with the Leatherback, it transpired, were three sea-angels, or swimming sea slugs, as Sophie whispered to Bob and Felicity. They floated upright and glowed in the murk, with two little pointed horns on their heads, a slug-shaped body, and what looked like delicate tapered wings on their backs. The tops of their heads and tips of their tails glowed red, while the bulk of their bodies was an icy blue, with a yellow tinge to their 'wings' and neck.

They were quite pretty, Felicity decided, although she grimaced as one of the sea-angels trailed sticky slime over her eyes. She blinked through the goo, then stared in wonderment. She could see properly in the dark! The sea-angels glowed brighter than before and she could clearly see their dragon friend again, along with Bob and Sophie and the Leatherback.

'Not a very pleasant sensation with the slime, but

effective for giving you the sight – and without the lantern effect, either,' said the sea dragon. Noticing Felicity's expression, he added, 'The sea-angels have given you enhanced underwater vision without enlarging your eyeballs. Much more refined. You'll likely see examples of the more goggle-eyed look down below later, where eyes loom large and luminous!'

Felicity was glad they didn't have bulging eyes, but she was sure that if that's what they'd needed, then that's what they would have opted for.

The Leatherback turtle worked its own peculiar magic on them, swimming around them in a way that looked almost as if it was dancing, before resting one of its strong front flippers on each of their heads in turn. As it did so, Felicity felt heat coursing through her body, a flare of warmth which settled down into a comfortable temperature. She guessed that was their ability to withstand the extreme cold sorted. Seven ridges ran down the length of the Leatherback's body, which had no shell, only this tough rubbery skin. They were instructed to lay their hands across these, and as soon as she did, Felicity felt something fizzle through her fingers, up her arms and down into her chest.

She felt different, but she couldn't have described in what way. This must be to protect them from the pressure of the water down in 'The Deep', she guessed.

'Leatherbacks can trace their ancestry back millions of years,' said the sea dragon. 'They have ancient wisdom and powers here in the Fairy Realm. Now, I think that's you finished.'

It was. Felicity, Bob and Sophie thanked the sea dragon for all his help – and the Leatherback and sea-angels – then fell in beside the kindly giant turtle, which had yet to utter a word, and followed it into the ocean.

***

Infused with fresh energy and renewed determination, Felicity and her friends followed the silent Leatherback eagerly, taking in their surroundings more keenly with their supercharged sight. It kept up a steady pace and, though they grew tired, the turtle encouraged them to hold onto its ridged back from time-to-time, allowing the creature to pull them onwards. Magic kept their quiet companion down with them for longer than Felicity knew it would normally be able to stay in the depths, and she was very grateful to the enchanted aquatic kingdom for that. They really didn't need to be getting lost down here.

Sophie pointed out a squid with bulbous eyes but an almost invisible body, as it was completely translucent, while other fish floated past with similarly protruding eyes to help them see in the dark. Felicity was glad of their gift from the sea-angels, minus the big eyeballs. Day or night, they'd never have been able to see down here otherwise.

One passing fish even had a large see-through forehead shaped like a dome, its eerie swivelling eyes locked inside like a museum display. Another came at them with big blue eyes which reminded Felicity of a car's headlights, veering off to the side just before they collided.

On they went, past fish with fangs and spiny needles protruding from their backs and fins; past shoals of twilight fish heading to the surface to feed, and dodging any jellyfish the Leatherback turtle didn't scoff. They were, Felicity quickly discovered, the turtle's favourite food, and some of them looked a bit like plastic bags floating in the water.

They must have journeyed through the night, though it remained constantly dark now around them. With their enhanced vision, however, Felicity, Bob and Sophie could see all the creatures they encountered, luminescent or not, the water in their direct line of sight bathed in a silvery glow that was light enough to show them what lay ahead. Which, as far as Felicity could see, was water, water and more water. No rocks or reefs down here. Or mountains – yet.

At last, the Leatherback stopped and motioned with its flipper. They must have passed through the Twilight

Zone and reached the Midnight Zone, which was their drop-off point. Ahead, the water now glowed a blue-green colour, which seemed to come from the creatures floating round about. Here, it seemed they had to generate their own light to live by.

They thanked their guide, patting the giant turtle on the back, which it acknowledged with a nod before beckoning to Felicity with a front flipper. She drew nearer, resting her ear close to its head. The turtle seemed to sigh, but Felicity was somehow able to understand its guttural communication and she nodded gratefully. It turned then and left them, heading towards the surface.

'What did he say?' asked Sophie.

'That this is the Midnight Zone but that it's not as big as the Twilight Zone, so we should reach the Abysmal Realm soon,' said Felicity. She glanced at Bob, noticing how his and Sophie's eyes gleamed silver with magic. Hers must be glowing too. They would have to be careful going onwards, as their eyes might draw unsavoury ocean-dwellers to them. 'Will we go on or rest for a while?' she said.

Oddly enough, none of them were really very tired anymore, which Felicity put down to all that magic they'd been gifted. So, they waited mere minutes before setting off again, buoyed by the fact that they were getting closer and closer to the Riddler's secret lair.

***

They sensed their entry to the Abysmal Realm when an eerie stillness, unlike any they'd encountered so far, draped over them like a shroud. It had been getting steadily quieter as they travelled, with fewer creatures sighted along the way, and a strange sensation came over Felicity as they moved into what she guessed must be this new layer of the ocean.

She assumed the feeling that had engulfed them all was down to their bodies adapting to the increased pressure, which she knew by now would have crushed them, had they not been protected by marine magic.

They'd kept close to the seafloor, which was now utterly flat and desert-like. Here and there, however, elegant sea lilies swayed like mute ballet dancers as they fed from the water, while Felicity spotted a curious creature which looked like a goldfish, actually walking on the seabed. Sea stars were also scattered around and about.

Any creature they did see was moving very slowly, and they passed them quickly, keen to leave this rather haunted place behind. It felt as if they were in the eye of a storm, thought Felicity grimly. She knew the closer they got to the Mountain of Lore, the more wary they should be of potential spies and allies of the Riddler, and indeed, the witches.

Trying to keep the seafloor in sight, the friends found themselves swimming down into a deep trench cut out of the silt and sand, and wallpapered with snowy-white sea anemones. Worms writhed on the ground and Felicity was glad to see they weren't Bobbits, though they weren't very pleasant all the same.

Eels also slunk past them, giving Felicity a creeping sense of dread. They seemed a good fit for a witch's spy and she swam faster to get away from them.

Having swum through the night, the friends finally decided they should rest, as they needed to be at full strength for tackling the Riddler's lair, even with fortified bodies. Felicity also wanted to check Bob's map again, to see if it had altered any to show more of the seascape. A blot of colour up ahead soon revealed itself to be a thriving and sprawling coral community, and they all agreed it was a good place to stop.

Unlike Ghost Reef, Felicity was glad to see that this coral was resplendent in shades of yellow, orange, purple and red – colours which came from the coral structure itself as well as from the many creatures living in and around it. It was like a deep-sea enchanted garden, full of scurrying crabs and lobsters, shrimps and prawns darting between the coral branches that snaked out into the water.

Above them, shoals of fish flashed silver and blue, while tat marine worms and what Sophie said were sea cucumbers flourished underfoot in the sand and amongst the coral rubble.

The reef was like a living tapestry, the coral twisted into delicate tree shapes, with feathered fingers reaching out into the sea for food. Sponges grew alongside gaudy sea anemones and Felicity knew at once that it was the perfect place for a rest. She wondered if any fairies also lurked in the coral, for who knew what was at the heart of it? After the recent barrenness of the sea, it was quite a delight to behold – almost like a mirage in a desert, but most certainly real. The ocean continued to amaze Felicity with the wonders it revealed.

It was Bob who jolted her out of her daze as he waved the map in front of her face. 'It appears that trouble lies ahead,' he said. 'Apart from the obvious, it would seem that this particular part of "The Deep" is resplendent in the following: sub-marine canyons, rift valleys, sheer cliffs and … very active volcanoes. Amongst other things. And what's more – as usual, the map shows no clear route through all of this terrain, or indeed, alludes to where exactly these dangers are!'

It didn't sound encouraging but before Felicity could reply, Sophie butted in. 'Uh, guys,' she whispered. 'I think there's something over there in the sand.'

Felicity turned just as a large column of sand rose up before them in the shape of a giant cobra. It towered above the trio and appeared to be made entirely from the sand itself. Felicity gasped. The snake reared its head back as if preparing to strike, a forked sandy tongue flicking in and out of its fanged mouth. Its eyes glowed like hot coals.

'Get into the coral!' she yelled, and the friends swam as quickly as they could towards it, Felicity thankful it was so large and sprawling. It shook as the snake dashed its body against the living mass, sand smashing into the reef and breaking off chunks of coral, those thin arms still searching for food.

The reef shook, but held firm, sand blasting through the gaps and stinging their eyes. Felicity realised with sudden dread that they could quite possibly be buried alive in there – smothered by sand. Just what were they to do now?

Chapter Sixteen
An Unpleasant Discovery

The cobra did its best to get at Felicity, Bob and Sophie, but the assault on the coral lessened with every attempt to batter it. Sneaking a peek by edging closer to the outer framework of the reef, Felicity saw that the snake had dwindled down to a thin spiral of sand. It seemed that with every dash of itself against the coral, the sand collapsed out of it and couldn't then reform back into the snake. Whatever magic was controlling it thankfully had its limits.

Bob and Sophie joined her, watching as the column of sand finally dropped to the seafloor, a small mound all that remained of the terrifying cobra. Creatures which had also sought refuge in the coral began to re-emerge, including an angry-looking fairy whose limbs were as scrawny as the fine coral branches. Her hair floated around her like feathers and two small wings protruded from her back. She had legs where Felicity expected a tail.

'You must leave here at once,' she said sharply. 'You

almost had our home destroyed. We can't risk him coming back with anything else – and he won't, if you're not here.' Her eyes narrowed.

'You mean that *thing* was here because of *us*?' said Sophie. 'We didn't want it around either, believe me!'

'What do you mean "he" won't send anyone else?' asked Felicity, although she rather suspected she knew what was coming by way of an answer.

'Why, the Riddler, of course,' said the fairy. 'You *do* know his mountain is in these parts and he doesn't take kindly to trespassers?'

'How do you know we're on our way to his mountain?' said Sophie. 'I'm a keen biologist you know. We might just be here on a fact-finding ecological adventure!'

'Sophie—' said Bob, but he was too late.

'It is as I suspected then,' said the fairy. 'The cobra was clearly from the Riddler and your answer has just confirmed you know who he is and that you are en route to his lair. A fool's errand, but I'd rather you went on your way and left us in peace. We mind our own business down here and don't provoke the Riddler's wrath. He's a temperamental and possessive creature with a lot of magic at his disposal, so it's for the best.'

'We *will* be on our way soon,' said Bob, 'but I'm afraid my friends and I have been travelling for quite some time without rest, so we would appreciate your hospitality a little longer. We'll help clear up this rubble and will leave at the first sign of any more trouble from the Riddler. I agree that this was probably a warning from him, but he likely thinks we've already taken the hint and left, so staying a little longer won't hurt now, will it?'

He looked beseechingly at the fairy, who sighed. 'Okay,' she grumbled. 'But not *much* longer. You must be on your way soon.'

'Thank you,' said Felicity. 'Is there anything you can tell us about the Riddler's mountain?' she asked, as they started to clear up the mess. 'It's not ideal that he knows we're headed that way, so it would help us a lot if we had some idea of the layout of the place. We have a map of sorts, but it's not very accurate.'

The sea fairy pursed her lips, then seemed to give in to whatever internal argument she was having with herself. 'I have cousins who used to work for him,' she said, picking up a piece of coral. She held it against a snapped-off bit of branch and Felicity watched as she fused the two pieces back together.

'I'm a coral-keeper,' she explained, noting Felicity's curious expression. 'My job is to look after the deep-sea coral gardens and this is my current posting. Normally, it's just a case of keeping them clean and tidy and sorting out minor disputes between the residents. Sand cobras aren't usually part of the day-to-day.'

Felicity opened her mouth to apologise again, but the fairy waved her hand in dismissal. 'Anyway, sea fairies all have different jobs and when the Riddler took up residence in the Mountain of Lore many moons ago, some thought it would be advantageous to work for him. They left their traditional trades and joined his ranks, but, as I said, he is a very possessive and untrustworthy type and accused many of them of spying on him and of stealing, or planning to steal, his many potions, magic and enchanted artefacts. He trawls the ocean you know, as well as the land, for treasures which he simply hoards. He might use some of them – I don't know – but he's very secretive, so who's to say what he really does with them?

'Eventually, he let all his staff go and one thing he *did* do with his magic, was to ensure that the Mountain of Lore was well protected in the absence of guards by, well, *other things*.'

'What kind of *other things*?' asked Felicity.

'Well, the Mountain of Lore is surrounded by various natural defences, all of which have the potential to eradicate trespassers. From what I recall from my cousins' stories, he's now surrounded by the following.' The fairy counted them off one-by-one on her webbed fingers.

'Mud volcanoes – *active* volcanoes. The Pools of Despair. Super-hot vents. The Lost City – or parts of it anyway. Also, an array of creatures including sharks, huge hairy crabs, stinging eels and probably much more besides, lurking in various nooks and crannies. He gives refuge to unsavoury sorts who have been thrown out of their own families and territories for any number of foul deeds, using his magic to ensure they can flourish down in "The Deep", whether it's their natural habitat or not.

'So you see, it's really not a good idea to try to visit him, though it would be best if you move on from here quickly. His spies must be out and about. News of strangers travels fast, even in "The Deep".'

Felicity took all of this in with a sinking heart. She could see that Bob and Sophie had been listening nearby too and were trying not to look as downcast as she felt. But they had no other choice but to go on. Time was running out for the realm with the creeping darkness, and no matter how well everyone fought against it on land, they had to ensure the boundaries were fully sealed by rescuing the missing fairy folk and reversing the pebble magic her grandfather had used.

She thanked the fairy for the information and re-joined her friends once the worst of the rubble had been cleared. Thankfully, the damage had only been around the outer layers of the coral, and the fairy's healing powers had helped it get back to more or less as it had been before. They rested a while, each lost in their own thoughts about what lay ahead. The creatures of the coral left them to it and soon, Felicity suggested they move on.

The fairy waved them off with a relieved look on her face and then they were out on their own once again, eyes peeled for spies. Felicity knew they had some advantage with the darkness cloaking them. They had their fairy sight for seeing well enough in the pitch black, but other creatures had their own adaptations for coping with the gloom, and she knew that, as these were fairy waters, they should assume there were things down here with abilities the three of them couldn't begin to fathom.

***

They'd been swimming in silence for a while, agreeing it was best to keep as low a profile as possible, when Felicity thought she saw something spiralling in the water a little way ahead of them. She held her arm out for Bob and Sophie to stop, but when nothing else appeared after a few minutes, she began to think she'd imagined it. Maybe being marooned at the bottom of the ocean was like being lost in a desert, she thought – after a while, you started to see mirages and imagined you saw things that just weren't there.

They swam on across a barren stretch of flat ground, but something didn't feel quite right about it. It was quiet around here, but Felicity felt her sixth sense tingle. Was it her imagination, or was the seabed vibrating ever so gently? She was just about to tell Bob and Sophie to stop again when a column of smoke burst from the sand, a hair's breadth from her face. She gasped.

The ground was erupting around them, as if that first column had triggered something under the seafloor. The ground rumbled and coughed up plume after plume of what Felicity realised now must be some sort of gas, not smoke.

Large bubbles popped up from the seabed one-by-one, exploding upwards in frothy plumes that looked like smoke from afar because they trailed silt and sediment behind them from the ground. They rose up towards the surface in a higgledy-piggledy fashion, so it was impossible to predict where they might come from next.

'Best skirt around them if we can!' said Bob.

Felicity soon suspected this was another of the Riddler's traps, however, when the gas plumes, which she guessed must come from the volcanoes the fairy had spoken of, seemed to track their movements until they had no choice but to weave through them, hoping one wouldn't explode beneath their feet and send them shooting into oblivion.

Dodging the plumes used up energy Felicity knew they shouldn't be wasting, but it was all they could do. Out-swimming and out-manoeuvring them was the only option. She swerved left as an eruption threw a stream of gas in her path, dodging right again as another went off a couple of seconds later. Surely this would have to stop soon? She saw her friends were having just as much trouble as she was.

It almost seemed as if the gas plumes were directing them somewhere and although Felicity didn't like to think *where*, they had to keep avoiding them, so were forced along a route they had no choice but to follow. Finally, the plumes grew fewer and fewer, but in lieu of volcanic action, something more sinister appeared ahead of them.

'What on earth is *that*?' said Bob, pointing to what looked like a big black eye squatting in a hollow on the seafloor.

It was as still as death and looked just as uninviting. It appeared solid, but as they drew closer, Felicity realised that it lapped ever so gently against a shoreline made up of rows upon rows of mussels - crabs and the occasional lobster scuttling about amongst them. None ventured into the black centre, which, surrounded as it was by the creatures on all sides, had the appearance of a lake, albeit a toxic-looking one.

'Excuse me,' she said to a passing fish. It was pure silver and looked quite bored. 'What *is* this place?'

The fish looked at her with some hostility. 'If you don't *know*, then you shouldn't be here,' it drawled and swam slowly away from them.

'How rude!' said Sophie. 'What about him?' She approached a big lobster and asked it the same question, this time, receiving an answer.

'Pool of Despair. One of,' he said in a croaky voice. 'Do not enter if you value your lives. Full of brine – super salty. Sucks the oxygen from the water.'

As if to illustrate the point, a lone fish – not the unpleasant silver one, Felicity noted – started to swim across the pool, but it hadn't even made it halfway when it seemed to realise its mistake. By then, it was too late. Floundering, the fish turned to go back the way it had come, but its movements weakened, and slowly, it floated down towards the thick, black gloop, until it was fully immersed and sunk out of sight.

Felicity swallowed.

'Okay …' said Sophie.

Bob looked rather ill.

'Like I said. Stay away. If you value your life. First of many.' And the lobster scuttled away.

Chapter Seventeen
Pools of Despair

'Never mind the Pools of Despair – I think *I'm* going to despair if we don't get to the Mountain of Lore soon!' said Bob.

'The fairy from the coral mentioned that the Riddler's lair was surrounded by the pools, though, so we can't be too far away now,' said Felicity. 'We've already dodged the mud volcanoes and here we are at the beginning of the pools, by the looks of it, so what's left? More of these, some super-hot vents and then the dregs of a lost city. Easy!' She grinned at her friends, hoping she looked convincing, but thinking probably not. They still had a fair few troublesome things to face, but they had also already *dealt* with a lot of trouble, so hopefully they could conquer whatever lay ahead.

'Yeah, great,' laughed Sophie. 'Don't forget the sharks and eels and whatever other creatures are waiting in the wings too! Actually, I would quite like to see those. I just don't want to get eaten by them.'

'Let's just see if we can make it past these pools first,' said Bob. 'Look – there are dead crabs all over the place, and other creatures too.' He shuddered. 'It's more like a *death* pool.'

It was true. As Felicity looked more closely at the pool, being careful not to venture too near the edge, she saw spiny legs sticking up from the inhospitable mass – crabs which had succumbed to the thick saltiness that made it so deadly. She imagined there were all sorts of other things lodged in its centre and shivered at the thought of it. The temperature was slightly warmer close by the pool, which she found odd. Perhaps it helped to lure unwitting sea-farers to their end.

'Yes, let's go,' she said. 'I don't like this place at all. We can swim around it and look out for more along the way. As long as we don't swim *over* the pools, or touch them, we should be fine, right?'

It seemed as good a plan as any, but as the mussel-encrusted ridge of another Pool of Despair came into view shortly afterwards, Felicity's heart sank. Circling it, as if impatient for someone to arrive, were long dark eels, and she knew at once that this pool would not be passed quite so easily. These were surely some of the Riddler's creatures, waiting to apprehend them.

'Let's just skirt out around them as far as we can and hope they stay put,' she said to the others, trying to stay positive.

'I think it's too late,' said Sophie. 'I think they've seen us.'

It was true. The eels had stopped their restless writhing and were hanging vertically in the water, heads pointed towards the three friends. A split-second later, they were zipping towards Felicity, Bob and Sophie, rapidly closing the distance between them. No one needed to tell them to swim for their lives. They were already in motion.

Felicity raised her back fin to speed away from the eel headed in her direction. She thought there were about four of them but she couldn't be certain, and more might lurk on the other side of the pool for all they knew. She risked a glance back to see how her friends were faring, but without the use of a super-fast fin like Felicity's, they weren't as nimble as she was. Sophie seemed okay, though an eel was on her tail, but Bob was in much more difficulty and she watched with horror as an eel wound itself around his leg and pulled him back towards the Pool of Despair.

Her own eel was catching up on her, so Felicity veered quickly away from it and swam back the way she had come, speeding past her pursuer in a flurry of bubbles. Bob was almost at the ridge of the pool. She had to hurry.

Channelling all of her remaining strength, she sped on through the water, feeling it warm a little around her as she neared the deadly briny mass. The eel hadn't seen her, so intent was it on its task, but Bob had, and his eyes pleaded for help while he simultaneously mouthed 'no' at Felicity. But she just had to rescue him. She wouldn't let her friend die, especially not like this.

Felicity stretched out her arms and brushed Bob's fingers as he was dragged over the mussels and clustered shellfish. With one last pulse of energy she reached for him again, and this time, grabbed hold of his hand. She wrenched him backwards and sideways, swimming ferociously to the left of the pool.

The eel, which had only now realised what was happening, reacted too late, and Bob pinged out of its grasp, propelling the creature out across the pool, where it began to writhe as if it was being electrified. It sunk lower and lower towards the blackness, twitching less and less before finally disappearing into the viscous darkness.

There was no time to celebrate their victory, however, as Felicity felt a tug on her own legs and saw an eel attached to each. Sophie had been abandoned, the third eel now also on its way towards her.

Bob tried to pull Felicity from their grasp, Sophie joining him just as the third eel latched on. Unfortunately, the eels' combined strength seemed to be greater than her friends', as Felicity began moving backwards. Then, she remembered her sail fin. In her panic at being caught, she'd let it retract, but now she raised it again to full height, kicked her eel-clad legs and tried to propel herself away from them.

Nothing happened.

She realised, too late, that the sail must work best when she was already swimming, adding momentum to movement. On its own, however, it lacked the energy required to make it effective. What now? She certainly hadn't come all this way just to end up another casualty of the Pools of Despair. The Riddler really must be incredibly possessive and paranoid about his collection if he had this level of defence around his home. Which made it all the more crucial they find his lair and the mystery object within. The thought gave her renewed strength, and as they passed over the clotted mass of shellfish at the rim of the pool once again, Felicity let go of Sophie's hand and grabbed at the lifeless crustaceans. She seized the leg of a crab upturned on its back, twisting round to stab at one of the eels. It hadn't been expecting the attack and the surprise more than the force of assault made it loosen its grip on Felicity's leg.

Sophie, seeing what Felicity was doing, also grabbed some of the mussels and began flinging them at the eels. Felicity kicked out and managed to throw the eel she'd hit with the crab leg away from her. They were almost over the liquid part of the pool and she reached for Sophie's

146

hand once again. Sophie grabbed it and, with Felicity kicking herself forward, the remaining eel weakened by Sophie's mussel attack, and the combined pulling power of her friends, she finally felt herself moving away from the deadly mass of brine.

When they were out of danger, Bob and Sophie let go of Felicity and got rid of the second eel, which seemed to think better of continuing the ambush on its own and slunk off into the gloom. Nobody said anything for a few minutes. They just looked at one another, stunned.

'Okay – it just got a whole lot more dicey down here,' said Sophie, breaking the silence at last. '*What* was that all about? I mean, okay, I know it was the Riddler, but seriously – *what* is his problem? Why would anyone have eels waiting to drag people into those hateful pools around their home? Creepy, horrible little man.'

'Yes, he is that,' said Felicity. 'But he must have a lot that he needs – or wants – to conceal in that case, one thing being the mystery object we need to help the realm.'

'I just hope we find it if we make it that far,' said Bob, his brow furrowing. 'I can't let Butterkin stay wherever it is that he disappeared off to. But we're strong as a team, and as I've said before, Felicity – you outwitted the Riddler once, so I have no doubt you can do it again. With our help, of course.'

Agreeing that it was best not to linger any longer

around the Pools of Despair, the three friends continued on their journey after a quick rest, watching out for eels and other undesirables – and for more pools. The seascape shifted around them once more, becoming rockier and even more hostile, if that was possible, thought Felicity ruefully.

The rocks rose up from the seabed as they swam on, jagged columns protruding up into the water like crooked, accusing fingers. They were scattered haphazardly around them and made Felicity feel almost as if she was in a city, surrounded by skyscrapers, as the rocky structures grew larger and larger.

'Of course,' she murmured. 'This must be the Lost City the coral fairy told us about.'

'Didn't she, er, mention something about super-hot vents too?' asked Sophie, looking around nervously. 'I don't fancy getting fried down here.'

'Nor do I!' said Bob. 'So keep your eyes peeled. Look – that seems to be some sort of vent up ahead.'

It was true. As they moved deeper in amongst the rock towers, Felicity saw plumes of smoke - some black, some white - curling up from what she realised must be the vents. It was quite bizarre to see what looked like giant chimneys smoking at the bottom of the sea.

The 'smoke' rose from the top of the vents, so they were able to get close enough to the rocky columns to see that they were writhing with life. The water was warmer here, no doubt due to the volcanic activity around the vents, Felicity thought, and she saw all sorts of strange worms and fish, as well as colourful sea anemones and sea snails living in this Lost City. Tiny bright-orange shrimps with no eyes darted in and around the vents too.

It wasn't until they reached an area of jagged white spires which stretched up into the water far beyond their view, that Felicity realised they must now be at the heart of the city. The ocean had cooled again, although their magic protected the three friends from the extreme cold anyway. Creatures with wispy strands floating out from their bodies circulated these spires, which Felicity guessed were also vents of a sort. They were quiet and eerie and felt dangerous, though she could see no one around them who looked suspicious. Perhaps the fairy had been wrong about the other creatures guarding the Riddler's lair. After all, she had only told them stories she'd heard. She hadn't been here herself.

The spires were full of cracks and crevices, however – perfect little hiding places for mysterious aquatic creatures.

'The Riddler's lair lies beyond the Lost City, so we must be very close now,' said Felicity to the others, who were staring around them looking as intrigued as she felt. 'Will we stop here a while and make sure we know what we're doing once we get there?'

'My thoughts exactly,' said Bob. 'And maybe time for more grub as well, wouldn't you say? All this underwater adventuring is making me very hungry!'

'I wonder what time it is now,' said Sophie. 'Is it lunchtime, do you think, or dinnertime again? Who would know down here?'

'We would!' said a voice that was most certainly not Felicity's.

They all looked at one another. What, or rather, *who*, now?

As if reading their minds, a group of voices said: 'Time-tickers, tellers of time - cogs in the wheel!'

Something rattled in the spires around them, followed by a series of tinkling and clinking sounds, as if someone was winding up an old jewellery box – or a clock – thought Felicity. It seemed that the voices were about to formally introduce themselves.

Chapter Eighteen
The Mountain of Lore

At first, Felicity couldn't see what was making the noises, but it sounded as if lots of little coins were rolling through the fissures of the spires and so, she waited with Bob and Sophie to see what popped out.

The first one zipped into the water like a shot, a blurry fluorescent shape quickly followed by lots of other blurry fluorescent shapes, until the sea around them was filled with an assortment of differently-coloured creatures no bigger than buttons. Some were like little cogs, others twisted into coils; some were stretched thin and wiry, while others were compressed into cubes. They were quite bizarre.

'Who are you?' asked Felicity.

The curious creatures replied in unison. 'We are the Ticker-Tellers. The Ticker-Tellers. The Ticker-Tellers. Who are you?'

'I'm Felicity and these are my friends, Bob and Sophie.

We're on our way to, well, to somewhere important, and wondered if we could rest here for a short while?'

'Of course, of course, yes,' said the Ticker-Tellers together. 'The Mountain of Lore lies not far ahead. If it is there you go, the Ticker-Tellers bid you beware.'

The little creatures rattled and clinked in agreement, pulsing fluorescent pinks and yellows, oranges and blues and greens. They really were a sight to behold.

Sophie snorted. 'Yes, we've heard all about the Mountain of Lore and the Riddler who lives there. Nothing like making you feel welcome, is there?'

'Welcome, welcome. We welcome you,' said the Ticker-Tellers.

'Um, Soph, I'm not sure they understand sarcasm,' said Felicity. 'But I think we're okay to stop here a while.' She turned back to the fluorescent creatures, who had grouped together in a billowy cloud and were watching them with interest. 'So – ah – what do Ticker-Tellers do?' she asked. 'I've never met any before.'

The little creatures jostled against one another in excitement.

'We tick the time!' said one.

'We tock the clock!' said another.

'We mark the minutes – all the minutes,' said a third Ticker-Teller. 'Since they ticked into being – till they tock to a stop. We are the Ticker-Tellers – we tell the stories of the ticks!'

'Let me get this right,' said Sophie. 'You guys have been here since, what, *time* began? Are you immortal? That's pretty awesome. How *old* are you?'

Felicity didn't know what to make of the creatures, but it made her feel a little funny to be in the presence of such ancient beings – if that was, in fact, what they were. Bob just raised his eyebrows at her and Sophie. 'Good, good,' he said. 'So, you're very knowledgeable then, I'd say, and very kind to be so hospitable to us. Are you the guardians of this Lost City? Nice to know someone's looking after the place.'

The Ticker-Tellers tittered amongst themselves at that, then said as one: 'We welcome you, we welcome you. We mark the moment, note the time.'

A pause.

'Would you like some?'

'Some what?' asked Sophie.

The Ticker-Tellers tittered again.

'*Time,*' they whispered.

Sophie's eyes widened and even Bob looked surprised. Or perhaps he looked more aghast, thought Felicity in amusement. 'You sell time?!' spluttered the brownie. 'Surely that isn't allowed? Isn't possible?'

'Make time, take time, give time,' said the Ticker-Tellers. 'Tell time, buy time, eat time, waste time. But we don't *sell* time.'

Felicity beckoned to Bob and Sophie, who gathered round. 'If they're going to give us some *time* – I mean, it's a bit unbelievable, but this *is* Fairyland - then why don't we take it? I mean, *any*thing's possible in the Fairy Realm, surely, and it might come in useful.'

Bob looked uncertain. 'Perhaps. But time – you don't want to go interfering with time. Makes me wonder what mischief these Ticker-Tellers are up to.'

'We could maybe just take some and *not* use it? Have it as a back-up?' said Sophie. 'You never know, taking time now might *buy* us time at the Mountain of Lore, or you know, *freeze* time or something. Who knows?'

'I think Sophie's right,' said Felicity. 'It might just help us and we don't know what's waiting for us at the Riddler's lair. Bob – what do you think?'

The brownie rubbed his head and looked at the Ticker-Tellers, who had quieted and were watching them intently. 'I'm not sure,' he said, 'but I suppose we could take a little and see what happens. Just a very little, though.'

'Agreed,' said Felicity, and Sophie nodded.

They turned back to the odd creatures.

'If you're willing to give us some time, then we'll gladly accept – but just a very little please,' said Felicity.

She wondered what would happen next. Did time come bottled or bagged? Was it invisible? Heavy? Light? Was this *really* a good idea?

The Ticker-Tellers swarmed around the spires and then, quite suddenly, disappeared back into their strange home. Not a single one remained.

Or so Felicity thought.

'Look,' said Sophie, pointing at Felicity's shoulder.

A cog – no – a *Ticker-Teller,* inanimate, was attached to her clothing. Bob and Sophie had one each too.

'Our time,' said Sophie, eyes wide. *'Weird.'*

***

The entire Ticker-Tellers experience had been very weird indeed, but Felicity, Bob and Sophie managed to rest sufficiently at the Lost City without any further interruptions and moved on as soon as they felt able, glad to leave the place behind. Each wondered how much time they now had pinned to their persons, and just what it might mean if they were to use it.

'The Deep' was a strange and unfathomable place, thought Felicity, full of undiscovered secrets and ancient creatures which were both simple and extremely complicated; odd and fascinating and often, uncomfortable to be around.

The Mountain of Lore was at last within their reach, however, and so they had to focus on what lay ahead. They still didn't know what they were looking for in the

Riddler's lair and Felicity was a little anxious about that and trying not to show it. Her Granny Stone always said things had a habit of working out, and she really hoped that was the case here, otherwise they could soon find themselves in a whole heap of trouble.

***

The friends swam on, the dark silence of 'The Deep' forcing them to keep quiet too as they travelled. No one seemed to want to engage in idle chit-chat as the Mountain of Lore grew ever closer. Also, they couldn't be sure what was lurking in the gloom.

This far down, despite now having time pinned to them, each had given up trying to figure out what time of the day or night it actually was. Time seemed to play by different rules down here and Felicity was still thinking about what the Ticker-Tellers had said. Had they really been hinting that they had been around since the beginning of time? It was almost too much to comprehend.

She wondered, then, if that was perhaps the point. The little creatures were distracting her from what she really *should* be thinking about – the Riddler's lair. She wouldn't put it past him to have had the Ticker-Tellers appear so they would lose their focus. He was certainly sneaky enough to do it.

She was about to say as much to Bob and Sophie, but the words dissolved in her throat as a dark, spiky shadow materialised up ahead. They all saw it and they all stopped as its outline grew sharper.

'The Mountain of Lore,' breathed Sophie. 'We actually made it.'

For all their intentions of making a plan of attack back at the Lost City, Felicity, Bob and Sophie had actually only agreed on what they really had already known. They had to sneak in, find the magical object and sneak back out again. It sounded simple, but when they didn't know what they were looking for, how to get in or out, or what sort of magic and guards might be protecting the place, it was all a little too vague for Felicity's liking. But breach it they must.

The Mountain of Lore was a sprawling rocky mountain ridge which cut into the water like shark's teeth. Felicity was glad to see that so far, there were no actual sharks to be seen. The initial shadow they had spotted turned out to be the start of a rather grand and convoluted entrance to the Riddler's home, but at last they saw a steep pinnacle of rock rise up from the ridge like a needle. This, Felicity was certain, was the pulsing heart of the Riddler's fortress.

So absorbed were they all in gazing at it, however, that they realised too late their mistake. They'd forgotten to stay alert to danger and it was now encircling them. Yellow slits of eyes glared at Felicity and around them, the water stirred with trouble. Something swished next to her and Felicity bolted, Bob and Sophie on her tail. They would just have to enter the Riddler's lair whatever way they could – and fast.

The mystery creatures chased them further into the rocky grounds of the mountain, snapping and hissing at their heels. Felicity's heart was galloping and she tried desperately to see if there was any sort of entrance they could dart into. Bob and Sophie seemed to be doing the same, but with no luck.

The seascape was hostile and seemed to take every opportunity to slow them down, their clothes snagging on rocks, their bodies dodging outcrops that Felicity could have sworn hadn't been there a second ago. More tricks from the Riddler, she guessed.

She had just narrowly avoided yet another unexpected rock-face, which quite literally was a face made of rock - and an angry-looking one at that - when Felicity swam straight into a soft, squishy, meshy sort of substance.

'A net!' she gasped, too late, as she bounced back from the impact. Bob and Sophie slowed beside her as the net closed in around them and hauled them upwards.

'It was a trap,' said Bob. 'Those assailants must have been chasing us directly towards this all along! I should have thought of that. Drat, drat and double drat.'

'We can't have come all this way just to get caught at the end of play,' said Sophie. Her eyes narrowed. 'Wait, I didn't mean to rhyme, but I think we're out of time.' She shot Felicity a look of surprise at her second rhyme.

'It's what he does. Just because,' said Felicity. 'Makes you rhyme, all the time.'

'It is *sublime!*' crowed a voice from the ocean depths. 'Glad you could join me, under the sea – *Felicity.*' A laugh. 'Brought friends too - now, that really won't do. It's only meant to be me and you. But I'll certainly see what I can do …

'I can't promise tea, but let me see – I think I've a dungeon fit for three. I'll let you settle in and then, we can begin.'

'Begin – what?' said Felicity. 'I think I'd rather not.'

'Why, storytime, my dear. I believe there's *much* to hear!'

Chapter Nineteen
Worlds within Worlds

'Sorry, I should have warned you,' Felicity told Sophie with a wry smile. 'Bob and I have been known to get captured now and again when adventuring in Fairyland!'

'Well, at least we're not rhyming anymore,' said Sophie. She looked around the dungeon they'd been rather unceremoniously dumped in and her face fell into a frown. 'Though it's not exactly five-star accommodation is it?'

'Prisons don't tend to be, no,' said Bob matter-of-factly. 'However,' he continued, in a more upbeat tone, 'Per aspera ad astra!'

Sophie's fringe raised as her eyebrows shot up. 'Huh?'

'"Through hardship to the stars"' - I remember,' said Felicity with a smile. 'I suppose everything comes at a cost and if it's worth having, then nine times out of ten you can expect that it won't be easy to obtain.

'Now, let's get thinking before the Riddler decides to

drop in for that chat. Although, if he's still so very keen to find out what I learned from the land of the giants then maybe that's to our advantage. We can use it to bargain with him.'

'I suppose,' said Sophie, 'he's fuming that you outsmarted him, but also very keen to use what you discovered.'

'No doubt he could get up to all sorts of trouble if he knew the secret Felicity brought back from the Causeway,' said Bob. 'But I imagine that it irritates him a lot not knowing what that secret is, and he will do whatever he can to learn it and use it for his own ends. The Rhyming Riddler seeks power and knowledge above all else.'

'I don't think we should waste too much time trying to figure out his motives,' said Felicity. 'He is a trickster after all. I don't always think he even *has* a proper reason for everything he does. He's just greedy!'

'Our time!' exclaimed Sophie. 'Shouldn't we use it now and see what happens?'

'I don't know,' said Felicity. 'Maybe we should wait – figure out a plan first and explore this place a bit in case we use it too soon and waste it. Anyway, we only asked for a little, so we might not have very much and as Bob said, it could be risky meddling with time. Best to wait until we're in a tight – okay, a *tighter* – spot?'

She looked around their watery prison. One minute they had been in the net, the next, in this dungeon. The Riddler was obviously impatient to get talking with them, so he could appear at any time. They also couldn't be sure he wasn't watching them right now, either, but they couldn't just sit here. Thankfully, they weren't chained and Felicity whispered to her friends to be careful what they said, for fear of the Riddler spying on them, then they began inspecting their surroundings.

The dungeon had no light, but Felicity, Bob and Sophie could still see well enough thanks to their enhanced underwater vision. She suspected the Riddler probably knew this. It was carved out of rock, of course, and had a vaulted ceiling. Unfortunately, probing the walls failed to reveal any hidden doors or escape routes. All that was left was the ceiling, so Felicity swam up to have a look, though she didn't really think it would offer a way out either. The Riddler wasn't stupid enough, surely, to make it that easy for them. Anyway, it gave her space to think and so, up she went.

She trailed her fingers across the rock, which was rough and jagged. Peering closer, she realised there were shell-shaped spirals cut deep into it. Could they be fossils, she wondered? She swam on, slowly becoming aware of a sound like teeth grinding together – or perhaps, stone scraping stone. A thought struck her and she returned to the spot where she been just moments before. The spiral was slowly unwinding into the rock, revealing a small hole. Felicity moved closer and put her eye to the rock, which had now stopped moving. Her mouth dropped open.

She'd expected to see into another part of the Riddler's lair, but instead, found herself gazing at what could only be described as a whole other world. She knew it had to be somewhere else altogether, because the first thing she noticed was the complete lack of water.

The place on the other side of the ceiling wasn't under the sea, but was full of sky and earth and creatures scurrying around. Felicity was looking down on them so had a bird's-eye-view of the scene. She couldn't work out who these people were, and indeed, they weren't *quite* people, as she saw a creature which looked like a person from behind, but then turned to reveal a goat's face.

Others had human-like – or fairy – hands, but the hind-legs of a deer or a horse. Yet others had feathered wings, or the heads of wildcats, their bodies a jumble of parts, yet none were fighting and it all seemed quite civilised.

Felicity took all of this in in just a few seconds, as the spyhole began to close over as she watched, until the shell was once again in place, leaving an incredibly baffled girl before it. Not wanting to move away, in case she forgot where it was, Felicity beckoned to Bob and Sophie to come up. It took a few minutes to get their attention and then she whispered excitedly to them what she'd discovered.

'Would it work again, do you think?' asked Sophie.

They tried again, Felicity tapping the rock and even trying other fossilised shapes, but nothing happened.

'Curious,' said Bob. 'Perhaps this has something to do with your abilities, Felicity? It could be that the rock was attempting to communicate a secret to you.' He frowned. 'Worlds within worlds. I wonder …?' His eyes sparkled at Felicity and Sophie. 'I wonder if perhaps we are getting closer to discovering what we have to do here, at the Mountain of Lore? We need to find the object that will help us get Butterkin and the others back. Well, the Mountain of Lore is built from ancient *rock*.' He looked excitedly at them. 'Don't you see?'

Felicity stared at the brownie, her thoughts tumbling around until something clicked into place and she suddenly realised what he was trying to say. 'You think this rock is somehow linked to the pebbles and the places they took everyone to?' she said slowly. 'But how?'

'Well, the Pebble People's pebbles originated from *some*where, and the Ticker-Tellers implied that they've been here since the beginning of time,' said the brownie. 'If pebbles – little parts of ancient rock – can transport folk to strange worlds, then surely the original rock, in all its spectacular mass down here, can do so *much* more?'

'Wow,' said Sophie. 'That actually makes sense. I mean, not that anything you say *wouldn't* make sense, Bob,' she flashed him a grin, 'but it really does, doesn't it, Felicity?'

Felicity agreed. But how were they to use this new information to complete their mission? And, she wondered, how much of this did the Riddler know about?

'It could also explain why the Riddler's so keen to get his hands on the giants' secret,' she said thoughtfully. 'If he knows about all of this – which we have to assume he does by living here – then he could possibly have a way *into* other worlds, but no means of leaving them. Which must be incredibly frustrating for someone who seems so intent on knowing everything and *taking* everything for himself. He can see what's out there, but he can't get to it.'

Bob nodded. 'Imagine what havoc he could cause by venturing into these other worlds. We mustn't give away what we know.'

They all agreed on that.

'So, next question,' said Sophie. 'Do you think we can get into the worlds from here, then, and if so, how do we do it? Is this how we rescue everyone?'

'I think it must be,' said Felicity. 'But yes, the problem is in doing all of that. I don't know why the rock revealed itself to me before and I don't know why it won't do it again. And the Riddler could pop up at any minute.'

'Felicity – you could hear what the trees were saying, back in the Whispering Woods. Maybe you can somehow communicate with the rock too? Or hear it, or something,' said Sophie. 'Maybe your powers are connected to the elements. I mean, heck, your surname is *Stone* after all!'

Felicity thought about that. 'Yes, but my grandmother only adopted the surname because the pebbles took her and mum to the Human Realm. "Stone" seemed a more normal surname to have than "Pebble."'

Sophie looked undeterred. 'Still – I think I'm onto something. What do you think Bob?'

'I think I might agree,' said Bob. 'And it's certainly worth a try, at any rate. Let's hope the Riddler gives us some time to "settle in" while we attempt to crack this.'

Felicity wasn't quite sure how to listen to or communicate with ancient rock, but she did what she had done with the trees and laid her ear against the surface, not sure what to expect. Trees were living organisms, after all, and her mum had always told her they could speak, but rock? Surely it was just an inanimate substance.

As with the trees, at first, all she could hear was a sound like the sea when she held a shell against her ear, but Felicity closed her eyes and concentrated, clearing her mind. As she did so, the noise intensified and soon, she began to pick out all sorts of sounds – voices and footfalls, music and rumbling wheels – the sounds of other places, somehow locked within the rock. There was no one voice that stood out, though – no single personality, rock or otherwise, spoke to her. It was all just a jumble of sounds which she couldn't quite decipher.

'I hear things,' she whispered at last. 'But are they echoes? Real worlds? How on earth do we get to them?!'

'There must be a way,' said Bob. 'If there are peepholes in the ceiling mightn't there also be entries on the floor? It's all rock too and I know I was only examining the walls before.'

They looked at one another and then sank slowly to the floor, scouring it for trapdoors, though Felicity knew that might be a bit too obvious. She felt drawn to a particular area, however, and swam over to investigate.

She jumped as a shape materialised in front of her. The Rhyming Riddler grinned roguishly.

'Storytime, my dear – or did you forget?
You have tales to tell still, but I've watched you, and yet …
Though I'd hoped to extract the truth from your lips,
You've told me all with your fingertips!
You peeped through the roof and saw something new,
And now I think we will bid here adieu.
For the Mountain of Lore is named as such,
Because deep at its core – revealed by a touch,
Some can discover worlds within worlds,
A magic man – even a brownie; two girls.

"Lore" is a word which means "stories" and "tales,"
And my home borders places where no ship sails.
For so many years I've gazed but not travelled,
Watching and waiting, till the secret unravelled,
Of how to escape them when exploring was done,
I could find no way how – not a single one!
Until you, Felicity, appeared in the realm,
Despite your attempts, with you at the helm,
I know we can venture into places unknown,
Because you have the magic to return us anon.
Now – forget about storytime, we must be away!
Let's keep those tales for another day …'

And with that, the Riddler grabbed Felicity and before she could resist, he'd pulled her through the rock wall and into the beyond.

Chapter Twenty
A Galaxy Unfolds

Passing through the rock felt like sliding through cold velvet, the hard particles of the Mountain of Lore relaxing into softness to let them pass. Felicity could almost have enjoyed the experience, had the Rhyming Riddler's bony hand not been pinching her wrist like a crab's claw.

She struggled, but that only made him grip her more tightly, and sense suggested that it might be best to see where they ended up before trying to escape the devious magic man. Felicity would have to choose her moment when he wasn't quite so fixated on her.

Silence wrapped around them, a scent which reminded Felicity very much of the stale smell of the ghost train at the amusement park back home filling her nostrils and making her feel oddly reassured and apprehensive at the same time. And then the smell vanished and the silence evaporated, as they emerged on the other side of where they had been, water rushing in noisily around them.

Felicity was momentarily confused, until she realised she had somehow been stripped of the magic that had protected her in 'The Deep'. Her lungs wanted air. She couldn't breathe.

Panicked, she kicked her feet, the Riddler's hand still grasping her wrist, pulling them both upwards. Just as she thought she was going to burst from holding her breath, Felicity's head broke through the surface and she gulped in breaths of cool, sweet air. The Riddler surfaced beside her, similarly gasping. He slackened his grip as Felicity swam to the edge of what appeared to be a lake, though it certainly wasn't like the ones she was used to, as it was a shimmering mass of rainbow colours. She flung herself at last on dry land, aware of the Riddler doing the same beside her and finally letting go of her wrist.

When she caught her breath, Felicity properly studied her surroundings, and really, she wasn't quite sure what to make of it all.

It was twilight – that sort of half-light which wasn't quite day or night, but which was enough to see by once your eyes adjusted to it. Around them and above them the atmosphere winked back, a dazzling cascade of stars spread out across the sky. They shone bright and colourful, and it was this vibrant light, Felicity realised, which reflected down onto the lake to give it that shimmering multicoloured appearance

As she studied them, Felicity decided they must in fact be a mixture of both stars *and* planets. She saw a purple globe surrounded by an outer ring of violet, and a bright star with sparkling pink dust swirling around it, shooting light out in four directions. There were planets shaped liked discus encircled by pale white light, planets emitting coiled helixes of orange and yellow, planets brown and billowing – like earthy dust clouds – and planets, or stars, marbled with a fusion of colours that quite dazzled the eyes. Felicity stared and stared, the Riddler almost forgotten.

'Didn't expect that now, *did* you?'

She could sense the smirk on his face.

'I don't think anyone could,' said Felicity. 'Wait a minute – we aren't rhyming!'

'No, the magic here distorts things,' said the Riddler, a little huffily. 'But your rhymes are rarely any good, anyway, so at least I won't have to hear them.'

'I only rhyme because *you* make me,' spluttered Felicity, indignant. 'So if they aren't very good then it's hardly my fault. Anyway,' she brought herself back to the matter at hand. 'Where have you taken us and how do we get back to my friends?'

She looked again to the sky, with its patterned planets and pulsing stars, swirls of cosmic colour breaking up the blackness behind it all. Were those actual *universes*?

'Where *are* we?' she murmured again, more to herself this time.

'Neither here nor there,' said the Riddler. 'Out of "The Deep" anyway.'

'Well, I'd worked that much out,' said Felicity.

'We are at the in-between and here you see before you ...' The Riddler swept his scrawny arms wide, 'worlds within worlds, which are ripe for exploring.' He rubbed his hands together. 'I know you found the secret to returning from other realms at the Causeway of the Giants. I had my suspicions, but couldn't make the journey myself, so you weren't all that clever after all in withholding the information. I've been studying these other worlds for years, biding my time until I had the means to do so in person and return to my mountain safely afterwards. And so – here we are!

'Actually,' the Riddler gave Felicity a sidelong look, 'I don't really need you tagging along. I only brought you this far so you would hand over the magic that will get me back again. So – where is it?'

Felicity suddenly became very aware of the Causeway stones she carried with her. She'd given one each to Bob and Sophie too, so she hoped they had the sense to use them to get out of 'The Deep' and not wait for her. Things could be about to get sticky.

'I don't think so,' she retorted. 'I'm not just going to

hand you what you want after everything you've done. I'm not scared to be here, if that's what you think. Annoyed, yes, but I haven't come all this way just to give you what you want and get nothing in return.'

'Oh … a bargain,' said the Riddler, rubbing his hands again in glee. 'Interesting.'

The strange coloured light reflecting off him made the little magic man look even more luminous than usual, as he still wore his multicoloured tunic, which was as iridescent as the sky above them.

'Yes,' said Felicity firmly. A thought struck her then and it seemed so frustratingly believable that she had an inkling it just might be true. 'You say you've studied these places – the strange realms and lands that I suppose the pebbles take folk to if they happen to lift one in Fairyland?'

The Riddler paused, then nodded. 'The pebbles all have their origins in "The Deep",' he said, yawning, as if the knowledge somehow bored him. 'That's why the Mountain of Lore is a window into worlds within worlds, because my home is carved out of the very rock from whence your precious, piffling pebbles were chipped away from. Anyway, what of it?'

Felicity sighed. 'Well, for that reason I'm pretty sure that *you're* what we were looking for then. Back in "The Deep". The Enchanter said we needed to find an object from the Mountain of Lore which would help us locate the folk spirited away by the pebbles. We thought it was something like a … like a …Well, we didn't actually know what it was, but now I'm fairly certain it was *you* all along.'

She felt angry, suddenly. 'If you study these worlds all the time you must have seen fairy folk appearing in them. Why haven't you done anything to help?'

'Not my problem,' said the Riddler cheerily. 'Serves them right for being so stupid.'

'Right, that's it!' said a voice behind them.

Felicity and the Riddler almost jumped out of their skins.

'You'll tell us what you know and you'll do it now!'

Chapter Twenty-One
Cosmic Capers

'Who dares to make demands of me?' said the Riddler angrily, glaring into the gloom. 'Show yourself this instance! Or are you too frightened to challenge me face-to-face?'

A guffaw was his reply. The Riddler looked incredibly annoyed, but Felicity couldn't have been happier. She'd know that voice anywhere by now. Her friends had somehow followed them.

'We're certainly not scared of you,' said Bob, emerging from behind a clump of rocks Felicity hadn't noticed earlier in the dark.

'Well, you should be!' said the Riddler, eyes narrowing. 'Trespassing onto my property. Withholding information—'

'But you almost had us killed!' said Sophie. 'Back in "The Deep". That giant sand snake – and the eels!'

'Are you sure that wasn't the witches' handiwork? Or because of the dark magic infiltrating the Fairy Realm?'

demanded the Riddler. 'Oh no, just blame the Rhyming Riddler as always. Why would I try to "off" you when *she*,' he pointed a knobbly finger at Felicity, 'has something I want? Hmm?'

'Actually, he has a point,' said Felicity.

The Riddler smirked.

'Anyway, that was before,' she continued. 'This is now and I think we were about to strike a bargain?' She glanced at Bob and raised her eyebrows. 'What do you think?'

'We have little time to waste, so whatever is quickest,' said the brownie. 'Though I don't very much like the idea of giving *him* easy access to other worlds. Who knows what meddling he'll get up to?'

'I believe,' said the Riddler, 'that you have bigger problems at the minute than my travelling around and gleaning magic from places. What harm can one little magic man do, hmm?'

His innocent words were betrayed by the glint in his eyes, but Felicity knew he was right in one respect. They had to act quickly, find the missing folk and return to help the Enchanter, her mother and her Granny Stone. If the Riddler was willing to trade his knowledge for a Causeway stone, then they'd just have to do it in the meantime and deal with him later if he caused any trouble.

'Okay, here's the deal,' she said. 'Riddler – you tell us which realms or planets or worlds or, *whatever*, the fairy folk were taken to, and we'll trade you some of what I found at the Causeway of the Giants, so you can go off exploring.'

The Riddler hesitated, then nodded as Bob glared at him.

'There are a few conditions too,' said Felicity. 'One – you also have to show us how to physically get to these places. We can travel back ourselves, but we don't know how we get up there.' She looked to the heavens. 'And second,' she continued, as the Riddler opened his mouth to protest, 'you mustn't do anything harmful when you're travelling. Nothing that will damage the Fairy Realm or put others in danger. Agreed?'

The Riddler was all puffed up with indignation, but then nodded his head sullenly. 'Now my conditions,' he said.

'Wait a minute!' said Bob. 'Who said *you* get conditions?'

'Your friend asks a lot, *brownie*,' said the Riddler, poking Bob on the chest. 'Now it's my turn.'

'What do you want?' asked Felicity.

'Enough of a supply of whatever it is you have from the Causeway to ensure that I can travel widely,' said the Riddler. 'And a promise that you won't spy on me, follow me, or come near me again.'

Felicity, Bob and Sophie huddled together for a few minutes, then Felicity turned to the Riddler and stuck out her hand for him to shake. 'Now, show us where the folk have gone to and then I'll give over your travel pass.' She pulled the Enchanter's list of names from her bag. 'These are the fairies we're looking for.'

The Riddler laughed. 'That's of no use to me,' he sneered. 'I have no idea who is who or where they are. I only know that I saw folk drop onto planets and into places from time-to-time, so I can tell you where to go to find "folk", but I can't tell you where any one individual is! What do you think I am? A secretary?'

Sophie tried to hide a smile, though Bob looked as if he would quite like to clobber the Riddler. The Enchanter's list would help them in finding all who were lost, then, thought Felicity, but it wouldn't assist in pinpointing who was where, as her grandfather had hypothesised. Still, it was a minor quibble at this stage. At least he'd been right about everything else.

'Okay,' she said. 'That'll have to do then. As long as we rescue everyone, it doesn't matter in what order.' She gave Bob an apologetic look. 'So, tell us how – and where - they are.'

'Say please,' said the Riddler.

Now it was Felicity's turn to glare at the little man.

'Alright, alright. I'm getting tired of all this anyway,' said the Riddler. 'Let me show you.'

He fumbled at one of the many pouches attached to his belt and produced a golden orb. He flicked it open and a miniature version of the sky above popped up out of it – a projection of the planets and stars, though Felicity knew it couldn't possibly be all of them. She was right. The Riddler's contraption, which he cradled in the palm of his hand, had a variety of tiny levers which, when the Riddler moved them, rotated the projection to show new planets and stars. Some pulsed more brightly than others.

'The brightest ones are the places where there's been recent activity – where folk have appeared unexpectedly,' said the Riddler. 'Make a note of them and you have your second list!'

Felicity was about to ask how she could possibly know what the planets and stars were called, when she noticed that below each one shone what she supposed was its name, though they were very odd names indeed. She realised something else too.

'So it wasn't you that we needed after all, but an actual object, as the Enchanter said. You tricked me again!'

The Riddler grinned slyly. 'I'm helping, aren't I? And anyway – how do you think you would have discovered that this was what you needed, when it was on my person the entire time?' He waggled his finger at her.

Bob had conjured up a notebook and pen, and set to scribbling down all the names, working his way through the system of other worlds until the last lever had been moved and all the names noted. The Riddler didn't let go of the orb throughout.

'Now,' said Bob at last. 'How exactly do we travel to these places?'

'Something for something. Give me my reward and I'll tell you,' said the Riddler.

Felicity reluctantly reached into her bag and found the pouch of Causeway stones. She withdrew one and handed it to the Riddler.

'Well, well, well,' he said, studying it. 'A Causeway stone. Thank you, my dear.' He gave another smirk and then it quickly disappeared into one of his pouches. 'I trust you have tested these to make sure they actually work?'

'Of course!' said Felicity, indignant. 'You can trust *us* Riddler. Now, how do we—'

'Yes, yes. It's quite straightforward. At the in-between, what's the fastest way to travel?'

Sophie piped up. 'I don't know about the in-between but in general, light travels fastest, though you can't travel *by* it.'

'Right – and wrong!' said the Riddler smugly.

Sophie looked puzzled.

'You need to hitch a ride on some *light* waves. And before you ask, they're all around you.' He gestured at the lake, which continued to shimmer like iridescent fish scales. 'I fully intend to go to whichever place you are *not*, but you can watch me leave if you must. No following though,' he waggled a knobbly finger at them, 'or there'll be consequences. I've been much too helpful to you lot already.'

'Don't you feel better for being nice though?' asked Sophie.

'No. Now, enough of this talk. I have travelling and discovering to do and if I were you … Well, I wouldn't wait around when you have witches watching and darkness stealing over the realm. I assume that despite our bartering,' the Riddler glanced at Felicity, 'I only need one of these stones, so enough dithering!'

Felicity couldn't have agreed more. She felt uneasy about the witches who, she had to admit, she had almost forgotten about since they'd found the Mountain of Lore. And she was curious about what the Riddler meant by travelling with light waves. She just hoped this worked – that they could locate the missing folk at last, retrieve them and return to the realm above sea level, where she hoped her family was safe and good was triumphing over evil. Just what would they return to if they did, in fact, make it back?

She shivered and turned back to the Riddler, who was preparing to leave. She watched as he knelt by the rainbow lake and dipped his hand into the water.

'Passage to—' He mumbled the name.

Felicity hoped they weren't about to be tricked again, as the Riddler raised his hand, now gripping a boomerang-shaped rod of glowing light. Then, before she could ask what he intended to do with it, the little magic man was catapulted into the sky, whooping as he went. He looked like a shooting star as he travelled into the cosmos, the glowing light wave gradually growing smaller, until it was just a speck, and then nothing at all.

Chapter Twenty-Two
Cosmitia

It occurred to Felicity, as the Riddler made his exit, that they hadn't asked him about how to travel *between* planets or stars - or whatever the places were that they were headed to. Did the one light wave work for every journey, or did they have to return to this spot each time? She sighed. She supposed they would find out soon enough. There was something else she wanted to know in the meantime.

'How on earth did you two get here?' she asked Bob and Sophie. 'You were at the other side of the dungeon when the Riddler took me. You couldn't have had enough time to follow us before the portal sealed over.'

'Ah, but you see, we did,' said Sophie smugly. She tapped her shoulder and it took Felicity a minute to realise what her friend meant.

'You used your time from the Ticker-Tellers?'

'We did!' Sophie beamed. 'And what's more – it worked very well!'

'We were able to rewind a little time, so we went back to the point just before the opening closed over, and slipped through after you,' said Bob. 'It was a bit disorienting, and we surfaced a little further along the shore, but yes, it worked rather well.'

'We used *my* time,' said Sophie. 'It was more than enough. I just took it off and asked it what we wanted, and it worked! Magic really is pretty awesome.' She grinned.

'Well, I'm glad you're here,' said Felicity. 'I just hope this light wave travelling works for us.' Her brow furrowed. 'Though I suppose we could always rewind time again and bring the Riddler back if it doesn't.'

Sophie shuddered. 'He gives me the creeps. I hope we *don't* see him again. Anyway – where to first? I can't wait to explore the planets. Who knew we'd end up somewhere like *this*?' Her eyes shone almost as brightly as the stars overhead.

'Yes, who indeed?!' said Bob. 'I never knew such a place existed in the realm or, well, in between the realms as it appears to be.'

'I mean, one minute we're under the sea – at the very bottom of it, as far as you can possibly go – which was weird enough,' said Sophie, 'and the next, well, we're manipulating time and travelling through walls and ending up in the cosmos! And now **an interstellar** trip or two. How is planet earth going to compare with all this when we get back home, eh?' She shook her head, grinning.

Felicity couldn't help but grin back and she cuffed her friend on the shoulder good-humouredly. 'Yeah, well, that's hoping we *do* get back! We've a lot to do before that happens, but I'm glad all of this isn't freaking you out too much.'

'Oh, it's freaking me out plenty,' said Sophie, 'but in a good way.' She seemed, then, to remember Bob's main reason for being there and added quietly, 'Let's see if we can't find Butterkin first. Do you have *any* idea where he could have ended up, Bob?'

The brownie shook his head. 'Sadly, no. The pebbles are quite unpredictable and none of us ever knew where any one would take you. That's why we always avoided them. It wasn't worth the risk of ending up somewhere horrible, but once they were moved around – and dropped – everyone was at risk.'

'Unfortunately, thanks to my family,' said Felicity.

'I don't blame *you*!' said Bob. 'It isn't your fault, or even the Enchanter's. Well, it's mainly his fault, but anyway, that's neither here nor there now. What matters is getting everyone back where they belong.'

'Hear, hear!' said Sophie. 'Now, where to first?'

185

***

Given the fairly lengthy list of names they had, and therefore places to visit to rescue everyone, Felicity, Bob and Sophie decided they would go to the first few places themselves, and then ask those they rescued to help them find everyone else.

'It makes sense,' said Felicity. 'Otherwise it'll take forever and there's only so much luck we can have. What if something happens to us along the way and no one else gets rescued? And,' she looked at Sophie pointedly, 'we're certainly not splitting up. We can ask folk who were spirited away to the more pleasant places to help, and hopefully they'll be willing. Plus, they're fairies, so they'll have a certain amount of magic they can use to protect themselves. Is everyone okay with that?'

Bob and Sophie nodded. Without further ado, they each dipped their hands in the lake and said in unison: 'Passage to Cosmitia!'

None of the names had held any obvious meaning for any of them, so they'd opted for one which sounded a little less likely – they hoped – to be a place of darkness and evil, though there really was no way of telling where they might end up.

'"Cos" – makes me think of "cosmic",' said Sophie, so they all agreed to try Cosmitia first. Felicity couldn't help

186

but think that perhaps it was another magical masquerade. The names were all more like nonsense words, so you still couldn't choose whether you travelled to somewhere good or bad. How on earth could anyone, for instance, guess what the following places were like? Czeces, Resynd, Peryle, Frologra, Pandol, Grebles, Ventaria, Snuffm, Jectur and of course, Cosmitia. Impossible!

As soon as they uttered the magic words, Felicity felt the water bubble around her fingers, then parts of it turned solid and she felt the boomerang shape of a light wave take form in her hand. She glanced at Bob and Sophie, then gasped as the light wave pulled her up into the glittering sky and off towards Cosmitia.

***

Felicity, Bob and Sophie sped through the sky at a lightning rate, or rather, Felicity hoped her friends were speeding along behind her because she couldn't turn her head to look, what with the rush of air blasting in her face. She couldn't hear anything because of it either. All was blurry around her, flashes and sparks whizzing past on the periphery of her vision.

After a while she heard a pop, which Felicity guessed meant that she had entered a new atmosphere, and she drifted down to the ground as if by parachute. It was a very odd way to travel and she was very glad the journey was over. She gazed around as Bob and Sophie plopped down beside her. At least the high-speed travelling had dried their clothes off after the lake.

The first thing she noticed about Cosmitia was that it was quiet, but then, after the noisy journey, anywhere would seem quiet after that, Felicity reasoned. Indeed, as she grew better accustomed to her surroundings, she realised there was actually a faint but constant humming and whirring noise in the background, and when she looked up, she quickly found the source of the sound.

Stilt-like structures stuck into the ground, which was yellow and crumbly like soil as opposed to sand, supported an array of tracks busy with all kinds of vehicles. Shaped almost like a rollercoaster, the tracks carried transparent cuboid vehicles on wheels, long rectangular carriages like those from a train and, quite unbelievably, Felicity thought, folk cycling along on rather grandiose Penny Farthings. She remembered seeing a Penny Farthing once at a museum and had often wondered how people in times gone by had climbed on and off them, given the extremely large front wheel. She supposed that here, it was less of a problem, as the creatures she spied riding the bicycles had long wings tapering down their backs.

Alongside the tracks were various brightly-coloured buildings and further away, Felicity could see lots of spired rooftops all huddled together like witches' hats. She guessed that was where these folk must live. The inhabitants of Cosmitia, meanwhile, all had bottle-green skin and black hair, and wore vibrant clothes. Felicity decided that it seemed like quite a cheery place.

Sophie echoed her thoughts. 'Well, as first impressions go, I'm pretty impressed. Seems safe enough to me? A good choice for our first destination! But – how do you suppose we get up there to look for whoever's stranded from the Fairy Realm?'

'I'm not sure, but at least they should be easily spotted, as they won't have green skin,' said Felicity. 'Although, actually, we can't be certain of that!'

'Look,' said Bob, pointing to one of the stilt legs. 'I think there's a ladder over there. Maybe we can climb up?'

'Good spot,' said Sophie, jumping up and dusting herself off. 'Let's go and see who we can find.' She glanced at Felicity. 'What should we do with these?' She held up her light wave.

'Just keep them handy, I think,' said Felicity. 'We don't know how quickly we might need to get out of here, so I think it's best to have them ready to use at a moment's notice. We all remember the name of the next planet, in case we have to make a quick exit?'

Bob and Sophie nodded. 'Great. Let's go then.'

They trudged over the mustard-coloured soil and found, as Bob had said, a long thin ladder trailing down one of the thick stilt legs.

'I'll go first,' said Felicity. Sophie got in behind her, followed by Bob, and they began to climb. It was higher up than Felicity had thought, but they finally reached the top and stepped onto a red wooden balcony.

'Don't look down,' murmured Sophie.

Up here, the view was much better, and Felicity saw a bustling city suspended in the air spread out before her. None of the folk took any notice of them, except for a few curious glances. Felicity was glad. She wanted to find whoever had been spirited here from the Fairy Realm as quickly as possible, so they could get on their way again.

It was daytime, and the light cast upon the place gave everything a yellowy tint. Wheels whirred around them, bells clanged and, up here, voices could now be heard as folk went about their business. They decided, that as everyone looked friendly enough, they would just start asking if anyone had spotted a visitor or two recently. However, it soon became clear that that wasn't going to help them, as no one seemed to understand a word they said.

'They speak another language,' said Felicity in dismay. 'I never even thought of that! Now what'll we do?'

'We'll just have to get looking – and fast,' said Bob. 'Someone definitely came here and we need to find out who!'

'Would it be rude to just start calling out?' asked Sophie.

'I've got a better idea,' said Bob with a grin.

He started singing a jaunty tune, which was catchy and basic enough that Felicity and Sophie soon picked it up. Felicity guessed it must be well-known back in the Fairy Realm and thought it was a very good idea indeed. Anyone from Fairyland would surely recognise the song and come to see who was singing it.

They walked along ribbon-like paths beside the tracks and through small plazas stretched across junctions, singing and scouring the vicinity for non-green-skinned folk. Felicity hoped it wouldn't take too long. The planet's inhabitants might be ignoring them, but she felt unsettled nonetheless.

They stopped after a while to rest their voices and themselves for five minutes and it was then that Felicity felt a sharp tug on her sleeve.

Chapter Twenty-Three
Peryle

Felicity turned, but oddly, could see no one. She frowned.

'It's okay – I'm invisible,' said a voice at her ear, making her jump. A hand clutched her arm again. 'You *are* here to rescue us, aren't you?'

'Yes, of course,' said Felicity, finding it difficult to speak to someone she couldn't see. 'Assuming you *are* from the Fairy Realm and got whisked away here by –'

'Pebbles. Yes, that's us,' said the voice sadly.

'How many of you are there? And, if you don't mind me asking, why are you invisible?'

'There's three of us. We made ourselves invisible because we stuck out like, well, like pixies with bright red hair in a land of green-skinned folk with jet-black hair! They aren't as friendly as they may seem, you know.'

By now, Bob and Sophie were listening in.

'Well, at least we've found you now,' said Sophie. 'We don't need to stick around here anymore then, do we? It might help if we could see you, though.'

Felicity sensed the pixies' reluctance to reveal themselves, but they slowly faded into view before them, three worried-looking folk with shocks of red hair which did, admittedly, stand out quite a lot in this place. She quickly explained their plan about finding the missing folk and asked if they would be willing to help them retrieve some more fairies.

'If you find folk in a pleasant place, then you can recruit them too,' she added, 'so we should find everyone much more quickly and all be back in the Fairy Realm sooner rather than later.'

'Unless you're too scared, of course,' said Bob matter-of-factly, 'in which case we'll send you off home now, where you can explain what we're doing.'

Felicity inwardly thanked Bob for his genius. The pixies hadn't looked very keen to help, but she could see the idea of being seen as cowards was even less appealing to them.

'We'll help!' they said. 'We have our magic as well and we might end up in a pleasant place, mightn't we?'

Felicity just smiled. Once she had distributed the Causeway stones, however – one for each of them and some extra for any folk they might find – she realised they had a problem. 'You don't have any light waves,' she said with dismay. 'The Causeway stones will return you to the Fairy Realm but we were told that light waves are the only way to travel between planets and places in the cosmos.'

The pixies and Bob muttered amongst themselves for a while, until at last, Bob informed them that the pixies should be able to replicate light waves from the three they already had by using their magic, though it might deplete the power of the new waves, as well as the existing ones.

'So, they may only find they can travel to one further location and we ourselves might find our travels restricted,' he said. 'It might not affect them that way, but we have to assume there will be some dilution of the magic.'

'Couldn't we just give them one of ours?' said Sophie. 'I'm sure I could share with Felicity?'

More discussion ensued, until Felicity remembered their time magic and it was decided that Bob rewind time with his Ticker-Teller, so he could return to the rainbow lake and collect more light waves. They held their breaths as he vanished, only to return triumphant mere minutes later, gripping a light wave in each hand.

'I couldn't work out how to get more,' he explained. 'The lake only seems to give up waves if you dip a hand in – and I only have two of those! But at least the pixies now have their own wave, which they can replicate for themselves and for the fairies they find.

'If they recruit more folk and *they* travel and recruit others, then they need only make one trip anyway, so the magic should be enough.'

Before they departed, Bob also asked the pixies to replicate the light waves belonging to him, Felicity and Sophie, so they had spares, which Felicity put in her bag. 'At this rate, we should all be back in the realm in no time, I hope,' she said. 'Oh – one last thing Bob. Can you cast a spell over our list to show the places that have been visited, so we don't all go the same ones?'

'I think so,' said Bob. 'Pixies? One more favour? Can you help me make a few copies of our list please?'

And so, they duplicated the list of planets to pass on, and Bob made it so that once a name was spoken, it would signal that it had been visited and everyone would know not to go to that place. With everything finally sorted, the two parties of three took their leave of one another, gripped their light waves and whispered their onward destinations. The pixies vanished first.

'Passage to Peryle,' said Felicity, Bob and Sophie, and the light waves whisked them away.

***

An ear-splitting shriek heralded the trio's arrival on Peryle, which positively trembled from the noise. Clutching hands to ears, Felicity, Bob and Sophie tried shouting to one another above the din, but couldn't make out what anyone was saying. Then Sophie pointed at something above them, her mouth hanging open in surprise, and Felicity saw what was making the sound. It wavered now, and quietened a little, before sliding into a deafening crescendo. It was, she realised, some sort of song, and it was coming from the mouth of a very tall, very thin woman, who scraped the sky, so high did she tower above them.

Piano music now joined in with the vocalisations and Felicity spied a tiny grand piano and player at the woman's feet. The singer, meanwhile, was draped in a flowing dress of ice-blue silk which fishtailed into ruffles at its base, folds swirling gently on the ground as if the garment was alive. Further up, it clung to the female's figure, which reminded Felicity of an upside-down vase – a very fragile, porcelain vase which might shatter at any moment.

Up and up the dress went, ending at a pair of skeletal shoulders, hands like talons clasped to a bosom which shuddered with every effortful breath needed to sustain the singing. The woman's head was thrown back, but Felicity could just make out a gaping mouth, sharp nose tip and darkened eye sockets as she warbled on and on. A fiery bob ended at her jawline.

The giant singer was surrounded by velvety-black sky sprinkled with pale turquoise music notes, which hovered lazily in the air around her like strange stars, pulsing and bobbing and streaming, Felicity realised suddenly, from the woman's mouth. The tiny piano player was but a silhouette below, but appeared to be bald. His coattails hung out over his stool and his arms were stretched long towards the piano keys, where his fingers scrabbled frantically over them.

Looking around, Felicity noticed nothing else, just darkness lit by luminescent notes and that tall icy lady. A tall icy lady who suddenly stopped singing, lowered her head, and stared Felicity right in the eye.

***

The silence was almost as deafening as the singing which had preceded it. The piano player played on, until he realised he was on his own, then snatched his fingers from the keys as if they had scalded him. The notes, which had been bobbing beside, above and around the woman, now tumbled slowly out of the inky darkness like snowflakes, drifting down to shatter upon the ground, which was black and smooth and polished. Anger flared in the singer's eyes as she flipped her head back again and began a new song, though Felicity still couldn't make out the words.

The notes began to rise once again, though they clinked and clashed against one another, as if in response to the rather venomous tone of this fresh tune. The song was sung low and soft, but carried with it an undertone of threat and malice. Felicity looked questioningly at Bob and Sophie. This place was on their list, so someone from the realm must be here, but who and where? She wondered if anyone else even lived here, for who could withstand the seemingly constant loud singing that was already getting on her own nerves?

Felicity moved away from the woman, gesturing at her friends to follow. They would just have to explore the place as best they could and hope they were able to find whoever had been sent here. She glanced back at the singer. Though her head was thrown back, her hollow eyes tracked the trio into the darkness.

***

The singing didn't stop, but it quietened a little the further they retreated from it, until Felicity, Bob and Sophie could at last hear one another if they each spoke very loudly indeed.

'Where is everyone?' shouted Sophie. 'Or does no one but *her* live here, do you think?'

'*Some*one must be here, *some*where!' shouted Bob, looking confused.

There was something decidedly off about the entire

place and Felicity felt that creepy, prickly feeling she couldn't shake come upon her. A tinkle sounded by her ear and she jumped. A crotchet hovered by her head. It seemed jittery, giving little jumps as if it was being electrocuted, which might, Felicity thought, have something to do with it having flown so far from the singer. She peered closer and as she did, the note blinked.

'What the — ?'

As she reached for the crotchet, it dodged away from her hand and Felicity took off after it, hoping her friends would follow.

'It *blinked* at me!' she yelled back at them. 'I think the notes are alive!'

She hadn't realised just how far they had strayed from the tall singing woman, but at last, Felicity found herself back where they had begun. The little crotchet disappeared into the throng of notes, leaving Felicity momentarily confused. Now what? Why had it led them back here? Was it just a trap? She'd suspected not when it came to her in such earnestness, but maybe she'd been wrong.

Then she had a thought. 'When perspective seems wrong …' she murmured.

It was a line from the Riddler's third and final rhyme when he'd set her those three riddles to solve on her first visit to Fairyland – before she'd realised she could come and go from the human to the Fairy Realm whenever she pleased. That line had referred to the Causeway of the Giants, but looking at the huge woman and the tiny piano player had made it pop back into Felicity's head. The perspective was *all* wrong here.

She'd assumed that what they were seeing was a giant warbling woman because of the incredibly loud voice and the odd scene before them. But they hadn't got very close at all to this singing sensation, and so, Felicity took a gamble and stepped forward. She did it again and again, racing past the piano player when she reached him, and then she was running towards the woman, breathless, and the singing was suddenly reducing in volume, the woman was slowly shrinking and the scene before her took on a very different perspective indeed.

For now there was a rather ordinary-sized female singing in a rather muted voice, and all around her were, not notes, but eyes. They blinked rapidly at Felicity as eyelashes grew out around them, and then noses and chins, foreheads and ears appeared. Necks elongated down into torsos next and finally, arms and legs and feet popped out to form full bodies.

The woman stopped singing, at last, and lowered her head to look at Felicity and her friends. She unclasped her hands from her bosom and extended a hand towards Felicity. 'My name is Peryle,' she said. 'And these are my children. However,' she paused. 'I always have room for more.'

Chapter Twenty-Four
Showtime

'I'm afraid we already have homes, thank you very much,' said Felicity, 'but we appreciate the offer.' She decided there was no point in beating about the bush now, as her Granny Stone would say, so she added, 'We've actually come to collect a friend who accidentally came here a little while back. If you could help us find them, we'd be very grateful.'

As she spoke, she scanned the assortment of faces around her, which were wearing all sorts of expressions and confusing Felicity as to their intent. Frowns, smiles and menacing looks were mixed in with shocked, aghast and frightened expressions. Really, any one of them might be from the Fairy Realm, but she suspected an angry or frightened face might be what she was after.

'My children are all the same to me,' said the singer. 'I love all equally and treat them all the same. They grow naturally in number, but I don't pick one out over the other. I couldn't possibly identify a newer child from one of old.'

'That makes no sense at all,' scoffed Sophie. 'How can you think they're all the same when they're clearly *very* different?'

It was true. The 'children' in front of them bore no real resemblance to each other at all, nor, indeed, to any creatures Felicity had seen before. There were various arms and legs ending in sharp points instead of fingers or toes, while some folk had noses made of flowers. A few creatures had ribbons for hair, others feathery fronds, while yet other children had cutlery where fingers normally protruded. Felicity spied a creature with tiny trumpets for ears, polished to a startling sheen, before spotting another with a coiled spring where a torso should be. She wondered how they kept their food down.

There was *one* similarity, however. They all had pearls for eyes.

'Who *are* you?' she whispered.

'I am Peryle and these are my words and my memories and my songs,' said Peryle. 'Some are adopted but most are of my own creation. Aren't they beautiful?'

Felicity just swallowed.

The children smelled of fruit and flowers, but also, of mechanical oil and dust and smoke. She felt sorry for these strange creations, but she really wanted to find their fairy and leave as soon as possible.

They couldn't free everyone else here, surely? Peryle

was small, but must be formidable if she controlled them and kept them here.

'Why isn't anyone coming forward?' she whispered to Bob. 'We can't just stand here talking all day – or night!'

'Maybe whoever came here has morphed into one of these creatures,' said Sophie. 'They might not know – or remember – who they are!'

'Sophie's right,' said Bob. 'They'll have been here a while, now, so the magic in this place could have altered them, though that doesn't mean it can be *un*altered. I hope.' He rubbed his chin and frowned.

Felicity wondered how the singer turned people into her children if she didn't birth them herself. She decided it was best not to look her in the eyes for too long, just in case, and whispered as such to Bob and Sophie. A thought struck her. 'Where's the piano player?'

'Do you think that's who we're looking for?' said Sophie, eyes lighting up.

'I don't know,' said Felicity. 'But it could explain why no one else is coming forward. Where did he go? I think it would be worth talking to him, at least.'

At that moment, the piano struck up another tune and Felicity whirled around. The piano player, however, was nowhere to be seen.

'You'll never find him,' said Peryle, a smug smile on her lips. Then she broke into song once more and with each note, she grew a little taller and moved a little further away from them.

'What now?' asked Felicity. Peryle's children began to sparkle around her again, once more becoming dazzling notes in the sky. Felicity tried to think. There wasn't very much to this place other than darkness, Peryle, her piano player – currently invisible or missing, but likely who they sought – and Peryle's twinkling, sort-of prisoner, children. Surely there had to be something she was missing? Fairyland was full of magical masquerades, tricks and deceptions, so she had no doubt that these other fantastical places they were visiting must be similar.

And then she had an idea. She turned to Bob and Sophie, who looked as if they were struggling to come up with any of their own.

'I think I have it,' she said excitedly. 'Or, I mean, I think I've thought of something that might help.'

'Go on – let's hear it!' said Sophie.

'Where do you usually see singers? Performers?'

'I dunno … a stage?' said Sophie, wrinkling her nose.

Bob's eyes lit up. 'Of course. She's a performer, even if only for herself and those "children", so she must be on some sort of stage. Therefore – '

'*We* have to go *back*stage and *there,* I think we'll find what we're looking for!' finished Felicity triumphantly.

'And, er, how do we do that?' asked Sophie. 'Won't we

have to get *behind* Peryle? Look how far away she is now. And I don't think she's going to come back and help us!'

'Unless,' said Felicity, 'we happen to use a little time that we have?' She tapped her shoulder. 'I still have my Ticker-Teller, so I was thinking we could conduct an experiment.

'So far, we've used our time to go backwards, but think of all the different types of time there are. Remember what the Ticker-Tellers said. They gave all kinds of examples of time – "make time," "buy time," "save time." So I was thinking – what about this? What about *showtime*?'

***

Sophie looked a little unsure, but Bob nodded slowly at Felicity's suggestion.

'Showtime – when the show begins, the curtain goes up,' he said. 'So, once we see where that is, we can get behind it and so, go "backstage," as it were. Maybe.' He scratched his head. 'It's a good idea, but there's no guarantee it will work.'

'But surely it's worth a try? I have nothing else, do you?'

Bob shook his head.

'Soph?'

'Okay - why not?' she said, grinning at Felicity. 'We

won't know if we don't try, and we're getting nowhere fast here at the minute, are we? What harm can it do?'

And so, that was that. Felicity unpinned her Ticker-Teller and held it in her palm, then did as Bob and Sophie said they had done with theirs and simply squeezed it tightly and asked of it what she wanted.

At first, she thought nothing was happening and then a soft gust puffed out her hair and suddenly, before them, hung a thick red curtain. It had worked and Felicity felt a fizzle of excitement. 'Quickly!' she hissed.

The three friends aimed for the left of the curtain, which was further away than Felicity had realised. Breathless, they pushed themselves onwards, regardless. If Peryle saw them, Felicity knew that would be the end of it all. Up ahead, a long golden cord was being pulled by a messy-haired fairy in grubby clothes, wings drooped rather despondently down its back. Was *this* their fairy that needed rescuing? The only one, or one of a group, Felicity wondered?

As they drew nearer, the fairy finally saw them, and his eyes brightened a smidgen before narrowing with suspicion. And then they were at the curtain, pulled now more than halfway open, and Bob was whispering in the fairy's ear and the fairy was looking relieved and Felicity saw at last what lay backstage.

Although she'd spent a lot of time by now in fairy

lands and magical places, Felicity realised she still thought of them in some way as being similar to home, just with added sparkle. Here, however, was a place which reminded her just how far away from home she really was.

Could a planet exist only as a stage? As a theatre? It certainly seemed so.

What Felicity saw behind the curtain was mesmerising in its madness. Unlike before, which had been all dark backdrop, sparkling notes and deafening Peryle, backstage was a kaleidoscope of colour as creatures darted here and there, each busy with something or other. They sprawled out as far as the eye could see, hundreds or more scurrying around trailing fabrics, necklaces, tall wavy feathers and even, Felicity saw with surprise, what looked like large foamy duvets.

There was no landscape in the distance, just miles and miles of workers and cubicles and partitions. Lofty wardrobes stood like skyscrapers here and there, while chests of drawers spilled out more fabrics and different-sized mirrors reflected it all back in a rather dizzying manner. It was chaos, but Felicity could almost begin to see a structure to the place, the more she looked. The furniture and the paths created by the folk made it look like a very strange sort of fabricated city.

'Unbelievable,' said Sophie. 'Is this like some sort of giant magical sweatshop?'

'Wait a minute,' said Felicity. 'With all these workers, it might be the sort of place we'd find Butterkin! I mean, I know he could have ended up anywhere, but it's possible. Bob said he's a cobbler, so I'm sure he'd fit right in here.'

Bob had returned with the fairy, who was indeed one of the missing folk. He told them there were quite a few others here as well, including the piano player.

'It seems that Peryle is a place – and, well, a person – which is quite adept at summoning or creating what it, or she, needs,' said Bob. 'So, somehow, Peryle's songs and music make her many children, who in turn, create costumes and scenery and all sorts for her various performances.'

'Self-obsessed or what?' muttered Sophie.

'And,' Bob continued, 'she can also fish them from other places. Passing travellers, people being spirited away by pebbles and so forth. She senses them and reels them in to be used for her own ends.'

'So it's possible that Butterkin could be here?' asked Felicity. 'She could make great use of him, no doubt!'

'It is possible, and yes, she could,' said Bob.

'So, how can we gather everyone from the Fairy Realm together without alerting all these other folk?' asked Sophie. 'This place is huge – will we have to trawl through all of *that*?' She swept her arms across the busy scene before them.

'Don't worry,' said the fairy. 'I can use a summoning spell. I'll put out a silent request for all fairy folk brought here by the pebbles to meet us and that should be that.' He looked at Felicity. 'Can you really get us back home?'

She smiled. 'We can – and we will. But first, your spell, and I think we'd better be quick, because folk are starting to stare.'

'Righto,' said the fairy. He looked at them nervously. 'Peryle will be livid when she finds out what we've done, so I hope we can exit quickly. You really don't want to be around when she unleashes her rage!'

Chapter Twenty-Five

Peculiar Horizons

All in all, there were eleven fairy folk trapped on Peryle, but still no sign of Butterkin. Felicity saw Bob was trying to hide his disappointment and she smiled at him reassuringly.

'He's hopefully somewhere a lot more pleasant than here,' she said. 'Maybe some of the others have already found him by now. He could be back in the realm for all we know!'

'I hope so,' said Bob. 'But it feels like he's still out there, somewhere.'

'We'll find him Bob, don't you worry,' chipped in Sophie. She looked around them. 'If that's everyone from here, though, shouldn't we be off? I don't trust these creatures. I'm sure some of them have already scurried off to tell Peryle about us.'

Indeed, at that very moment the singing, which was miraculously very well muffled behind the curtain, stopped.

There was a pause and then Peryle's shrieks assaulted their ears as loudly as if she was right in front of them.

'Quick! We've got to go *now*!' said Felicity. She'd been distributing the light waves and Causeway stones, explaining what the folk had to do. Luckily, the fairies were able to duplicate the light waves easily. It had taken a little longer than she'd hoped to convince them to help, as most just wanted to return home as soon as possible, but in the end they'd agreed, and were now being vaulted skywards by their light waves, en route to more strange locations to rescue more folk.

The ground began to shake around them, mirrors cracking and wardrobes splintering. Slivers of sharp glass and spiky wood flew towards them like arrows, and Felicity paled. Peryle's shrieks were deafening and her children were grabbing hold of whatever was within reach to use as weapons against the three friends. She heard the curtain swish forcibly apart behind them just as she, Bob and Sophie yelled out: 'Passage to Frologra!'

The light waves whisked them upwards, but less quickly than before, and Felicity realised that Peryle must be using her powers to try and reel them back in. She willed the waves to be stronger, as they appeared to lose speed, but then, it was as if they had gone beyond the domain of Peryle's influence and they catapulted forward as if fired from a cannon.

They were on their way to Frologra.

***

Felicity had completely lost track of whether it was day or night, breakfast-time or lunchtime, as every place they visited had its own foibles and was governed by strange moons and stars and who knew what else. They were working through their list, however, and with the folk they were saving along the way also helping with the rescue effort, they were getting closer and closer to returning to the Fairy Realm – and to her family. She wondered how things were back there, but the places they visited allowed for very little reflection, as they were all challenging in their unique ways.

In Frologra, for instance, the place had been full of huge, slimy frogs, so spotting the poor fairy folk in amongst them hadn't been very difficult. The frog princess had been rather hospitable once they explained who they were and what their business was, but the few folk they found were very glad to leave the place behind, as it was green, extremely slimy, very chilly and very wet. They handed out light waves, Causeway stones and instructions and off they all went.

Snuffm was smoky and hot and uncomfortable, and smelled of spices and hay. The sky was crimson and the ground blackened, the inhabitants scaly-skinned and surly and arguing constantly amongst themselves, though thankfully, the thick smoke make it easy to hide from them. Felicity was sure she spied the black tips of witches' hats when they were there, so she was very glad when they found two fairies and were on their way again.

Bob had quickly learned the summoning spell from the fairy back on Peryle, which was, he admitted, much stronger than any *he* knew, so they were able to use this to silently alert folk to their arrival each time they landed somewhere new.

They found talking animals in Czeces who were friendly enough, though Sophie couldn't quite believe they all lived in brick houses and strode about the place in perfectly tailored clothes in a most civilised fashion.

Jectur, on the other hand, seemed to have no inhabitants at all, save for the one unfortunate fairy they found there, who had gone half-mad with all the white light and vast space and strange, coloured bubbles floating in the air. It smelt like strawberries, so wasn't unpleasant, just oddly eerie and unsettling, and Felicity could see how it would drive anyone over the edge if they stayed there for long enough. They sent the fairy straight home with a Causeway stone.

None of them knew how quickly time was passing as they were whisked from one place to the next, but at last, Felicity checked their list and realised they had just one location left to visit, thanks to the help from their rescued fairy friends.

That place was Grebles.

Grebles stank.

As soon as they landed, Felicity, Bob and Sophie scrunched up their noses in disgust, as their nostrils were flooded with the stench of rotting meat and matter. It was as if every bad smell Felicity had ever encountered had come to live in the place, except here, there was no fresh air to blow it away. It took every effort not to gag. Sophie wasn't quite so lucky, as she promptly threw up.

'It's the eating quickly in between journeys, and the lightning-fast travel and now this *reek*!' she gasped. 'It's beyond gross! There are no words to describe how disgusting this place is!'

'It *is* foul,' said Bob, his arm across his mouth muffling his words.

Felicity thought everything about Grebles was awful. It was cold and grey and stinking, with mean little clouds nailed into the sky and huge swathes of wasteland sprawled around them. Beyond that was a forest of naked firs, their branches bare of needles. The trees were very close together and looked prison-like, Felicity decided, the trunks more like bars made for trapping people. After that, there appeared to be a grey city on the horizon, which looked as uninviting as the rest of the place, but they decided that was their best bet in finding any sort of life. It did, however, mean they would have to go through the foreboding forest.

Buoyed by the fact that this was their last destination,

however, Felicity had a bit of a spring in her step as they walked. That was, until a shadow flitted across the sky and the air began to hum. The humming morphed into moaning and Felicity's skin grew cold. It couldn't be, could it?

No one had to suggest running for, as one, they broke into a sprint, hurtling towards the trees. What cover could the strange forest possibly provide though, thought Felicity worriedly. They had to weave through it, which was awkward, but quickly answered her unspoken question. If they stood still, they would be hard to spot amongst the skeleton trunks, so closely together were they. She told Bob and Sophie to stand against a tree and then, they waited.

The moaning had intensified overhead and shadows swept across the forest as something passed by above them. They each hugged their trees closer, pressing their faces to the trunks, until the shadows were gone and the moaning faded, as whatever it was moved further away.

'What was *that*?' said Sophie, trembling.

'I've no idea, but let's hope they don't come back,' said Felicity. She paused. 'Bob – you don't suppose they were b –'

'Banshees? No, I think not,' said the brownie. 'But something similar, I think, by the sounds of it.'

Having saved them from encountering whatever had miraculously passed them by, the skeletal forest, Felicity decided, was no longer quite as threatening as it had seemed before. It offered them some sort of camouflage and for that, she was grateful.

They met no one in the forest, which trailed down to the grey city like a cluster of skinny dominoes, so regimental did the trees stand in the soil. It was as if the ground itself was decaying, Felicity thought to herself, which would explain why the trees looked so ill. They snacked on a few biscuits and water along the way. In truth, none of them felt like eating, thanks to the rancid aromas around them, but they agreed that they needed to keep their strength up.

At last, they reached the edge of the forest, the city no longer a grey blot in the distance, but rising up ahead of them like a creature which might just bite their heads off, should they venture too close to it. All remained eerily quiet, but Felicity knew better by now than to think that meant there was no one – or nothing – around. They knew someone from the Fairy Realm must be trapped in the city. Now, they just had to find them and get out of here.

'Bob – can you do your summoning spell?' she asked.

He nodded, and she and Sophie waited while he performed the magic. It was quickly done.

'Now, we wait,' he said. 'Hopefully, we might not need to go in there.' He glanced at the city with disdain. 'I can only imagine the smells *inside* the place when it reeks so strongly outside it!'

Sophie tried, and failed, to conceal a smile.

They waited for quite some time at the fringe of the forest, then they waited some more. They waited and waited, until Felicity decided enough was enough.

'We have to go in,' she said firmly. 'The spell hasn't worked for whatever reason, so we'll just have to risk it.'

'Are we sure there's definitely someone in there?' said Sophie.

'It's on the list we got from the Riddler,' said Bob, frowning, 'and it's been right every other time.'

'Maybe there's magic here which is affecting the spell,' said Felicity. 'Or maybe it'll only work inside the city.' She studied its walls. They looked cold and uninviting, and beyond them it probably stank, as Bob had suggested, but Felicity knew they couldn't just give up now. How would *she* feel, she wondered, if it was her in there and her would-be rescuers decided at the end that they'd saved enough people, so missing one last one wouldn't matter? No, they had to go in and give it their best shot.

'We'll just stick close to the walls and stay alert,' she said. 'We'll find a safe spot for Bob to try the spell again and if it still doesn't work, then we'll just have to go exploring.'

'Well, it *is* what we do best!' said Sophie, grinning.

Once again, Felicity was glad to have Sophie with her.

She was a welcome splash of home in an otherwise strange and hostile place. 'Okay – let's go,' she said.

They made a run for it, heading for the smoky-grey wall wrapped around the city, and towards a gaping archway which looked like the way in. Darkness gobbled them up as they darted through it.

Chapter Twenty-Six
The Gliders of Grebles

Inside the city of Grebles the air was stale and cool and reminded Felicity of the smell that lingered in old wardrobes full of forgotten clothes. Musty it might be, but at least the foulness from outside somehow hadn't punctured this silent space. That didn't really make her feel much better about what she saw, however.

'It … It's a *graveyard!*' said Sophie. 'A graveyard city? A city with graves? What *is* this place? And who lives here – the undead? Actually –'

'Let's not go there,' said Felicity, glancing around nervously. 'This place is seriously creepy, so I think we should stick close together and do what we have to do as quickly as we can. Bob?'

The brownie was pale as sheep's wool, but nodded. 'Best we find a safe-ish nook and then I'll do the summoning spell.'

Around them were tombs of all shapes and sizes, scattered like birdseed across the interior of the city. Some rose tall and statuesque, while others hunkered to the ground like wild animals ready to pounce. Cracked paving wound around them, while from black mulchy soil grew grey-stemmed flowers with red thorns and smoky petals rimmed with red. Petrified gargoyles squatted amidst all of this, their bulbous eyes seeming to follow them, Felicity thought, shivering.

The place was full of nooks and crannies but they chose a corner near the entrance, behind a stone creature Felicity couldn't identify. It was large, and had fangs and bat-like wings, so was intimidating enough that she wasn't keen to take a closer look. She crouched beside Bob and Sophie as Bob performed the spell. He had just uttered the last word when an almighty crack rent the air, making them all jump – and Sophie yelp in surprise. It shook the city and a low rumbling started up around them.

'That sounds like—' Sophie began.

'The noise from earlier,' finished Bob grimly. 'Something's on its way.'

The rumbling changed to humming, the humming morphed into moaning and the moaning melted into wails which really did make Felicity think of the banshee she'd encountered in the Fairy Realm once before. They huddled together as shadows flitted across the tombs and statues, stirring the stale air and sending shivers down Felicity's spine.

'I think they're searching for us,' said Bob. He was

peering around their statue, which thankfully hid them well enough in the corner. So far, anyway. 'The spell I did must have alerted them. Maybe magic isn't allowed here, or they can just sense it.'

'Well, this place seems pretty dead and gloomy, so I imagine whoever owns those shadows isn't a big fan of spells fizzing with energy and aliveness,' said Sophie.

'I just hope whoever we summoned from the Fairy Realm has the sense to hide and not give the game away,' said Felicity. 'What if —'

She gasped as something slammed into her side, knocking her to the ground. Whatever it was pulled away from her as quickly as it had attacked, however, and hovered above them, waiting. Felicity heard Bob and Sophie exclaim behind her.

The thing was like a giant inkblot – black, fluid and flying.

Huge bat-like shadow wings protruded from the creature's similarly shadowy body, which otherwise, didn't appear to have a distinct head, neck or indeed, arms or legs, though two curls of black spiked the sky above where its head might have been, two eyes of gold burning beneath.

'We have to get out of here!' Felicity hissed, pulling Bob's sleeve, as he seemed transfixed by the thing before them. '*Bob!*'

But Bob was staring at the shadow creature, his eyes

bright with unshed tears. He extended his hand towards it and whispered: 'Butterkin?'

***

Felicity had never been so dumbfounded in all her life. This couldn't possibly be Butterkin the brownie, Bob's missing best friend. It had to be some kind of trick from this place, to lure them into whatever deadly trap these creatures had laid. And yet …

As she looked back to the creature she saw that it too had eyes bright with emotion and she saw sooty tears drift to the ground as it stared at Bob.

'What have they done to you, my friend?' whispered Bob. 'I'd know those eyes anywhere.'

'The summoning spell must have worked after all,' breathed Sophie. 'But can we take him back like this?'

That seemed to snap Bob out of his stupor. 'Of course we must take him!' He turned to Butterkin. 'We'll find a way to fix you, I promise, but you're coming home with us.'

Too late, Felicity realised the wails were encircling them now more loudly than before. A flock of shadows was almost upon them.

Before she could call out to Sophie, Bob or Butterkin, the keening phantoms glided down and smothered them

222

in a cold, dark embrace. It chilled Felicity's very bones and she blacked out.

When she came to, her friends had gone.

***

Felicity bit back her frustration as she couldn't believe they had been captured at the very last place on their list before returning to the Fairy Realm. It was the worst possible luck, although at least they had finally found Butterkin, albeit in phantom form. She wondered where her friends were. There was no use in having found Butterkin if they were all now prisoners. *That* was no help to him at all.

It was dark as a crypt, which, it dawned on Felicity, must be where she was, as there was wall at her back and the only structures they had seen outside had been tombs. She swallowed, and felt around to see how large her prison was. She could stand up, though her head brushed the ceiling, and she counted ten steps lengthwise and seven across. Definitely a tomb then, though at least she hadn't stumbled across a coffin.

A stone ledge ran down one length of the tomb and Felicity lowered herself onto it and thought. A zig-zag of moonlight splintered the darkness from a crack in the wall. She had felt smooth cold stone on all sides of the tomb – no doorways – but she decided she wasn't going to panic just yet.

Felicity focused on the moonlight, as there was nothing else to look at, and as she watched, she could have sworn it was expanding. She blinked, but there it was – a lightning bolt of silver that was rapidly growing on the floor of the tomb. She could do nothing but watch in amazement as the light took form and she saw the silhouette of a large hare.

'Are you ready?' said a voice.

'Um – ready for what?' asked Felicity. 'Who's there?'

'I am your designated Moon Hare,' said the voice, soft as silk and almost hypnotic. 'I lead the dead to the afterlife and here you are, ready to be led.' A pause. 'You *are* ready, are you not?'

'No! No, I am not!' spluttered Felicity. 'I'm not dead and I'm definitely not ready for the afterlife, thanks all the same. I'm here by accident – my friends and I were captured by those shadow things.'

'The Gliders of Grebles,' purred the voice. 'Why haven't they eaten you by now, my dear? Perhaps they are occupied with devouring your friends?'

The voice didn't sound mean, nor did it appear to take any pleasure or indeed, displeasure, at the words it spoke. In fact, Felicity rather got the impression that this Moon Hare was indifferent to the outcome of her and her friends' predicament altogether. So, she took a deep breath and spoke calmly, quelling her anger.

'What do you mean by Gliders – and eating people?'

The Moon Hare sighed. 'The Gliders of Grebles are the phantoms, or shadow creatures, that you speak of. This is their domain. They feed on flesh and souls – I take what remains to their final destination. If they consume flesh, I transport souls. If they suck the souls, then I dispose of the flesh outside the city.'

'So that explains the stink,' muttered Felicity, her stomach heaving. She felt sick. 'But no one else lives here, so who do they eat?'

'They travel when they must – by mist,' said the hare. 'But they can last years without consuming anything. Perhaps that is why they have not eaten *you*. Perhaps they seek to grow their numbers?'

'You mean, turn me into one of them? I don't want to be stuck in this place, or live off flesh and souls, thank you very much! As you can see, Moon Hare, I'm still very much alive, so if you could help me get out of here, I'd be incredibly grateful. If you must take me somewhere, then let it be away from here, and to my friends, so I can rescue them and get back to the Fairy Realm.'

Silence hung around them like a ghost as Felicity awaited the hare's response.

'Follow me,' it said at last.

'Er, how?' Felicity couldn't see any way out of the tomb and she certainly wouldn't fit through that crack.

'I travel by moonlight,' said the hare. 'Stand in my shadow and you will come with me from this place.'

The only thing Felicity could see was the silver hare-shaped outline on the ground, so she supposed that must be the hare's shadow. She rose from the ledge and stepped into it.

At once, she felt as if she was spinning – like she used to do in the garden at home, head tilted back towards the sun as she spun giddily around, only to crumple in a dizzy heap when she inevitably fell over. The sensation was the same, except now, Felicity was spun by the moon and twirled into an altogether different sort of place.

The tomb fell away and she stumbled, almost losing her balance as she felt wide open space around her. Shrieks pierced the air. The Gliders must have sensed her escape. They would hunt her down and then what? Felicity didn't want to hang around to find out.

Chapter Twenty-Seven
Mist and Moon

The Moon Hare had brought Felicity to a part of Grebles she hadn't yet seen, a place swirling with a thick misty vapour that obscured all around it. She couldn't see any Gliders, but that didn't mean they weren't out there, lying in wait.

The mist was laced with moonlight, so she saw the hare properly for the first time. It was completely black and cast a silver moon shadow on the ground.

'Here is where you will find your friends, if they are still to be found,' said the hare. 'At the place where the mist and moon mingle – where things transition and shift shape. It is the best I can do.'

The Moon Hare stared at Felicity with luminous silver eyes, then turned and vanished into the fog.

Felicity was alone again, but at least she was no longer trapped in a tomb. The Gliders might travel in mist, but it also helped to keep her hidden, so she began to walk quietly through it, searching for signs of Bob, Sophie,

Butterkin and, of course, the phantoms. The mist was cool and quiet and strung diamond drops of dew through Felicity's hair.

Something whooshed past her, to the left, ruffling the air and making Felicity jump. A Glider? She could see nothing through the haze. Her heartrate quickened and she tried to steady her breathing.

Another whoosh, this time to her right. Perhaps the Gliders were toying with her before they sucked her soul out, or turned her into one of them. Felicity thought that maybe now it was time to properly panic.

She had frozen to the spot at the last whoosh, but now took another tentative step forward. She was determined to find her friends. Further into the sea of mist she went, each step more purposeful than the last. After a while, it was as if something was leading her in a specific direction, though all around was only steadily thickening mist, with no route visible.

'Oh!' said Felicity, bumping into someone.

'Felicity? Is that you?'

'*Sophie*?'

'It's her! Thank goodness we found you. The summoning spell worked!'

That explained her purposeful walking then. Felicity could just about see the outlines of her friends – and the blackish blob that was Butterkin – and she grinned.

'Did you meet a Moon Hare too?' she asked.

'A moon *what*?' said Sophie. 'We managed to wriggle away from those phantom things – no offence Butterkin – thanks to brownie number two.'

'And now that we've all found one another again I think we should use our Causeway stones and get back to the Fairy Realm at last!' said Bob.

'I couldn't agree more,' said Felicity. 'These Gliders of Grebles are *not* really my cup of tea. No offence Butterkin. Will he—' She looked to Butterkin. 'Sorry, will *you* be okay coming back with us in this form? I mean, I'm sure the Enchanter will be able to help turn you back.' She thought she saw Butterkin do a sort of nod.

'We'll just have to see what happens,' said Bob. 'But we'll get you back to your brownie self, Butterkin, I promise. Now, let's get going.'

They each took out their Causeway stones, Felicity handing a spare to Butterkin, who grasped it in a shadowy wing. Then she took Sophie's hand and Bob reached out for Butterkin – just in case – and they asked the stones to take them back to the realm.

The mist swirled around them and the moon shone bright, as Felicity, Bob, Sophie and Butterkin winked out like a light.

***

Felicity had travelled many ways within the Fairy Realm, and now outside of it, but she thought the Causeway stones' magic was perhaps the least unsettling of them all. Perhaps it was because their purpose was to take folk home again that it felt as if someone had wrapped you up in a warm hug, sung sweet stories in your ear and filled the air with the blossomy smell of spring. Felicity felt snug and safe, her mind pleasantly fuzzy, as if on the cusp of sleeping or waking.

It was, however, a sensation that didn't last for very long. She felt her feet touch the ground again and her travelling cocoon fell away like a dream. Instantly, she returned to herself and opened her eyes to Fairyland.

A plump moon beamed brightly overhead, drenching the copse where she stood in its silvery glow. Encircling the grassy space like solemn sentries, were tall pine trees that were growing so closely together, all Felicity could see was a darkness even the moon seemingly couldn't shift. It was as she imagined the skeleton forest in Grebles might have appeared, if it hadn't been devoid of pine needles. Behind her, hugging the perimeter of the forest, was a thin stone tower which rose like a poker just a little above the pines.

It was quiet. *Too* quiet. Where were her friends and why was she here?

Something dropped down behind her and she swung round to see Sophie opening her eyes and looking a bit bleary-eyed. She grinned when she saw Felicity.

'Made it!' Her eyes did a quick sweep of the copse. 'Made it *where,* though? I thought we asked the stones to take us to your family?'

'We did, but I'm beginning to think the stones have a mind of their own,' said Felicity. Not *great* at following instructions, are we?' she said to her Causeway stone, which she then pocketed.

Felicity rubbed her eyes. She couldn't remember when she had last slept. She sighed. 'On the other hand, it's more likely that someone's meddling with the Causeway stones' magic – someone who's been keeping track of our movements ever since we left and has been waiting until we returned to the realm.'

'Er, someone like witches?' asked Sophie, glancing around uneasily.

'Yes,' said Felicity. 'Exactly like witches. They've had enough time by now to work out the secret of the stones and they probably realised how my family returned anyway, after capturing my mum and Granny Stone with theirs. They haven't brought Bob and Butterkin here though, if it *is* them doing all this.'

'Divide and conquer,' said Sophie, frowning. She glanced around again.

'Unless they're in *there* somewhere.' She pointed to the firs. 'Doesn't look very welcoming, does it?'

'No. I vote we try the tower. We can at least get a bird's-eye-view of where we are from up there.'

Sophie spun round, her eyes widening when she saw it. 'I'm up for that! Well, as long as there are no spooks or witches in residence.'

Felicity hoped it was empty too, but there could be something inside that might explain why they'd been brought here. It was worth a try, anyway. Good or bad, they had to find out. Without further ado, the pair approached the building, which had a sliver of door and just one window at the very top, unless, Felicity mused, there were more at the back of the tower, on the tree side. The window was in the pointed roof and was quite a way up.

The door was made of heavy wood and had a large rusty handle. It creaked loudly in protest when Felicity pushed it open, allowing just enough space for her and Sophie to slip through one by one. Immediately behind it was a flight of steps. The tower seemed simply to be a staircase wrapped in stone. The question was – just what would they find at the top?

Chapter Twenty-Eight
Tower Trouble

'For a place full of magic they really could make better use of their powers, don't you think?' Sophie puffed as they climbed. 'I mean, haven't they heard of escalators?'

Hopefully we aren't too far off the top now,' said Felicity. It *had* been quite a climb and her legs were aching. The stairway was dark, due to the lack of windows, so when moonlight started spilling down the steps ahead, she knew they must be approaching the tip of the tower. Her legs felt heavier and heavier as she forced them up those final few steps, her body yearning for rest and seeming to grow wearier as an end to the climbing beckoned.

She stepped into the small circle of room, Sophie close behind her. It was empty. A crow perched on the window ledge. It cocked its head, then took off into the night, calling something back at them. It was a pity, Felicity thought, she didn't speak 'crow'.

Something shifted underfoot, making the tower tremble. Felicity glanced to the doorway, but there was now no entrance to be found, just solid stone all around them. She realised their mistake too late.

'Witches,' she murmured.

'What? Hey, where'd the door go?' Sophie spun round in a circle only to see what Felicity had seen. No door, just stone. They were trapped.

'That crow must have been one of the witches' messengers,' said Felicity. 'My brain's so foggy with tiredness and travel that I wasn't thinking when I saw it before. The witches must have manipulated the Causeway stones' magic as we guessed, to get us here and trap us. They've probably had eyes on us all along, thanks to those dratted crows and whatever other creatures do their bidding down in "The Deep".'

'Well, that octo-woman was creepy – and a cousin of the sea witches, wasn't she?' said Sophie. 'The giant sand serpent was probably the witches' work as well, then. And the Bobbit too, of course. Maybe even the *eels*! We thought all that was the Riddler's doing, but he did give a good argument about why it wasn't him.'

'The eels could still have been the Riddler's,' said Felicity. 'But Bob and I *did* get a warning from the witches when I arrived in Fairyland. I just thought we'd be somehow safer from them underwater. So, *now* what?'

'Well, we've done *our* part in helping to save the realm, so maybe your family is free by now? Bob and Butterkin will surely raise the alarm and come looking for us. Right?'

'I just hope they made it back okay,' said Felicity. 'But *we* did, so we'll just have to assume they did too. Right, I think we have some work to do!'

'Um, like what? Escaping?' Sophie peered out of the window. 'Hate to break it to you, Felicity, but we're currently stuck at the top of a tower in the middle of nowhere in the Fairy Realm. A tower which appears to be under the witches' spell, might I add. How on earth are we going to escape? I mean, I'll do whatever we need to do, but—'

'I need to think,' said Felicity. 'One thing the Fairy Realm – and Bob – has taught me, Soph, is that there's *always* a way. Always. You just have to figure it out, *especially* here, where the place is full of magical masquerades and whatnot.'

'They could have at least left us a chair or something,' grumbled Sophie. Then her jaw dropped. 'And what about other things – like going to the *toilet*?' Her eyes widened in horror. 'Okay, let's get thinking, or it could all start getting *very* gross in here!'

'At least we won't starve,' said Felicity, holding up her bag, which still held her magic crockery.

'Hmm, it's what happens *after* we eat that I'm worried about,' said Sophie, raising her brows. 'You know, Felicity, it's a pity we didn't find out anything else about what powers you might have. It would have been really handy if you knew a spell or two that would get us out of here.'

Felicity was disappointed as well that she hadn't learned anything more about her magical abilities, but she tried not to show it. 'Well, the Enchanter told me last time that I could return here to learn from him and develop my powers, so I get the feeling that they won't just appear all of a sudden,' she said. 'I'll have to work at it.'

'Like school,' Sophie sighed. 'But then again, *magic* school, so that's way better.' She grinned. 'Are you going to stay here for good, then – in the Fairy Realm?'

Felicity hesitated. She'd already discussed this with her mum and Granny Stone, but she hadn't really thought much about it during their adventures. Soon, however, the decision would have to be made.

'I'm not sure,' she said. 'My grandmother is coming back to be with the Enchanter and I think my mum would like to stay too, but she's willing to let us live part-time in the Human Realm, if that's what I want.'

'And *do* you want?' asked Sophie.

'Sort of yes and sort of no. I mean, that's where I've lived all my life so far, but half of my family is from *here* and even if I cross backwards and forwards to visit them, the time difference will mess things up.'

'If you stay for good then I'll never see you again,' said Sophie.

'Well, I could visit *you* and my dad,' said Felicity. 'Now and again. It might be easier that way around. And here, I could learn how to develop my magic and get to know my grandfather.'

'Sounds like you've decided, then,' said Sophie. 'I'm a bit – okay, a *lot* – jealous, you know. I mean, who finds out that they're from the Fairy Realm and gets to live there? Then again, who gets to see that Fairyland even exists, and travels around the place having all sorts of fantastic adventures?! So I guess I'm pretty lucky too.'

Felicity smiled at her friend. 'I just wish I could work out how to get us out of this tower.'

Sophie stuck her hands in her pockets and sighed again. 'There must be something. Wait a minute ...'

She beamed and pulled something out of her pocket. 'We forgot we had *this*!'

Now it was Felicity's turn to grin. Sophie held the glamouring ring Felicity had given her when she arrived in the realm, moonlight glinting off the stone like a charm. Mezra's gift was going to prove useful once again.

Sophie handed the ring to her friend.

'You can turn yourself into an eagle, or something

strong enough to carry me, anyway, and then we can get outta here.'

'No time like the present.' Felicity slipped the ring on and imagined herself as a small dragon. *That* should certainly be strong enough and it would give Sophie a surprise.

Nothing happened.

'I don't understand,' she said, frowning.

'Are you sure you're doing it properly?'

'I'm doing what I did the other two times I used it, but it isn't working. Maybe the magic has run out, though I didn't think it could. Mezra told me it wouldn't work immediately after being used, but that after a short while, it would be fine again.'

'Maybe being in "The Deep" messed it up? Here, let me have a go.' Sophie held out her hand.

Felicity took the ring off and handed it back to her friend. Sophie slipped it on and after a couple of seconds it began glowing, changing from red to green. She watched as the air around Sophie – and Sophie herself – started shimmering, her friend's features shifting and morphing into something else, something red and feathered, with thick yellow scaly legs, and talons that looked as if they could shred stone.

The bird – Sophie – almost filled the room as she flexed her wings, stretching them wide before tucking them behind her. She had a hooked beak and flowing tail-feathers which looked like red and yellow ribbons trailing on the floor. On her head sprouted shorter feathers which were an orange-yellow colour closer to her skull and tapered off into that vibrant red. In the moonlight she looked quite fierce but also, beautiful, magical and above all, strong.

'A giant phoenix,' breathed Felicity. 'Good choice, Soph. You know, maybe the witches don't realise you're here. It's *me* they've been after and they don't know what abilities I do or don't have, so maybe whatever they've done to stop me escaping with magic hasn't had any effect on you. Anyway, I'm just glad it's worked. Let's get out of this tower!'

Sophie, the ring sparkling on one of her curved talons, bowed before her friend, and Felicity carefully climbed up onto her back. The thought struck her, as Sophie perched on the window ledge before take-off, that her friend better be able to use those wings, but then she remembered how *she'd* been able to automatically fly when she'd once turned herself into a crow, and so, as Sophie stepped off the ledge and took to the sky, she simply held on tight and marvelled once more at seeing Fairyland from above.

They left the tower behind, flying over the pine forest and onwards into the realm - a slip of a girl with long amber hair streaming in the wind, astride a fire-bright bird – backed by the light of a silvery moon.

Chapter Twenty-Nine
Fairyland Re-stitched

The Fairy Realm felt alive beneath them, which is to say, every part of it that Felicity could see appeared to be glimmering or moving or flowing, energy pulsing through the land like a heartbeat.

Forests rustled loudly with the voices of ancient trees as they passed overhead; rivers tripped and fell over rocks and down mountainsides in even more of a rush than usual, though they spoke no language Felicity could comprehend. Small figures flitted from place to place, all seemingly headed in the same direction, but towards what, remained a mystery.

The copse where the witches had trapped them had been silent and still, perhaps muted by magic, Felicity thought, but now, Fairyland bubbled up around them, ripe with the sounds of night, but also, with the voices of excited fairy folk and of the very landscape itself.

Something was afoot but Felicity got the feeling that for once, that something was good, and her heart quickened as she realised that perhaps – just perhaps – they had saved the realm at last and had forced the dark magic to retreat. They had rescued all the missing folk, after all – the list had shown every location visited, anyway – so the borders of the realm should be healing and sealing over again. Once they had closed, Fairyland would be protected as it had been before from the ghouls and blacker than black magic that had been polluting the realm. She scoured the ground, wondering where Bob and Butterkin were in all of the busyness below.

'Keep going Soph, if you can,' she urged her friend. 'I don't recognise this part of the realm yet.'

On they flew, Felicity watching as Fairyland seemed to shake off the last lingering elements that had invaded its borders. They soared over woodland where warm lights flickered and eerily beautiful singing floated up around them, the fairy pipes and flutes much more pleasant to the ear than Peryle's music had been. Felicity remembered how Bob had told her that folk had been shutting themselves inside at night when she first arrived back in the realm, for fear of the creatures and the evil roaming when the borders were jeopardised. If the fairies were out and about again, then they must feel safe.

Of course, the Fairy Realm had its own share of dark creatures and shifty folk, not least the witches and goblins, but if the harpies and demons and who knew what else were still about, then surely the fairies would still be hidden underground at this hour?

Sophie flew steadily onwards. Phoenixes, Felicity knew from her books, were notoriously strong and she was fairly certain they weren't usually this big, although she only had half-remembered stories to go on, so Sophie must have wished herself as big as she could to help them get away.

Now and again, a slash of light – sometimes purple, sometimes pink, yellow, or fir-green – split the sky, accompanied by a sound like the cracking of a whip, but Felicity knew it was no lightning. On other occasions, it flashed for a second across a forest or a glen, and she knew that these cracks of colourful light must surely be Fairyland's hidden borders healing and making themselves whole once more. It made her heart sing to see it.

As they travelled, the moon's light began to wan, as dawn nudged her out of the way in favour of honeyed morning light which spilled forth across the realm like silk.

Felicity wondered when the fairy folk had last welcomed such a dawn, as she knew the dark magic had wreaked havoc with the seasons and had steadily smothered the light, plunging everything and everyone into more dusky darkness than was normal.

She still didn't recognise the landscape, though it was hard to identify places properly from her bird's-eye-view. Everything appeared flatter and ran into everything else in a most confusing way from this perspective. Below, was a patchwork of fields and woods and rivers which, at last, opened out into the sea, its salty aroma flooding Felicity's mind with thoughts of home. She asked Sophie to fly lower so she could try to work out where they were.

Felicity was studying the ground so intently, however, that she was paying no attention at all to the sky. Sophie, too, had her eyes fixed firmly below. That's why, when something crashed into them from behind and knocked them from the sky, it took the phoenix and her friend quite by surprise.

***

Felicity and Sophie fell into the waves lapping against a sandy cove. The water was icy-cold, which, along with smacking unexpectedly into it, stunned the two girls. They managed to make it the rest of the way to the beach, however, and collapsed, shivering, onto the sand. Sophie's soaked feathers made her look a sorry sight indeed, as they clung to her body, her long tail-feathers drooping like wilted flowers. She scrabbled at the ring on her talon but couldn't get at it properly, so Felicity helped pull it off and watched as the familiar form of her friend reappeared, still drenched, but now fully clothed.

'What on earth was *that*?' Sophie exclaimed. 'Did you see anything?'

Felicity shook her head. 'No, but whoever – or whatever – attacked us is probably close by.'

She glanced around the cove. It was small and curved inwards like a smile, blocking the view from either side, though Felicity was sure she remembered seeing only ocean either side of it before they fell. Ahead was a wall of towering rock, which seemed to offer the only option for exploring. She wasn't sure how long it would take for the ring to recharge, but at least they had that option for escape. So, their only immediate problem was the assailant who had brought them here. Her eyes searched the sky, but there was nothing but cloud.

'Let's check the rocks,' she said. 'There might be caves over there.'

'And things hiding in them!' said Sophie dubiously, but she joined Felicity nevertheless, approaching the rocks with caution. As they drew nearer, Felicity saw that there did indeed appear to be a cave inside the cliff, and so, she and Sophie inched quietly into the cool darkness.

They were only a little way into the mouth of the cave when bony fingers seized their arms and dragged them further inside. Before they knew it, Felicity and Sophie were securely tied up. A fiery torch flared and was held in front of them, dazzling the girls so they couldn't see their captors.

'Where's the phoenix?' a voice demanded. It sounded wet and gurgled, and Felicity wasn't sure if it seemed *very* threatening, although their being trussed up as they were certainly didn't reflect well upon its owner.

'*I* was the phoenix but as you can clearly see, I'm really a girl,' retorted Sophie. 'Was it you who shot us down from the sky? You could have killed us!'

'We knew the sea would catch you,' said another voice, also wet and gurgled. 'Wouldn't risk harming the loot, though now it seems we have no loot to harm!'

'Who *are* you?' asked Felicity, peering into the gloom. 'Can we at least see you? And why didn't you come out and get us if you were so desperate for your *loot*? We might not have even come in here, for all you knew.'

'Too many questions, but we'll show and tell.'

More light flamed around them as lanterns ignited en masse. One of the voices said: 'We prefer the dark. Dislike the sun. But fire is okay.'

'The sun *is* a great big ball of fire,' said Sophie. 'Why don't you like it?'

'Too much light. Too hot. Be quiet.'

Sophie *was* quiet then, as she and Felicity finally saw their captors. Glaring at them were two very tall, very gangly creatures who bore a striking resemblance to seaweed. It was the closest thing Felicity could compare them to, as she looked them up and down in amazement.

Their long bodies looked like the wavy, rubbery seaweed Felicity was used to picking her way through when she walked on the beach after a high tide. They were brown as autumn and looked slick and slippery. They each had a mop of what she assumed was what passed for hair, but which reminded her of sea anemones, while their arms and legs were stalk-like, with thick, bulbous toes and long, spindly fingers which resembled coral. That was why they had pinched so much then, she thought.

'We are Smugweeds,' said one of the two. 'We smuggle sea treasures and sky treasures and land treasures. We like the night and dark, damp, gloomy places, but often watch from our cave in daylight hours in case of missed loot. We shot you out of the sky with a clam and now we need to figure out what to swap you for, and whom to swap you *to*.'

'Swap us? I don't think so!' said Sophie, indignant. 'You must release us at once, or we'll set the Enchanter on the pair of you. That will put an end to your smuggling!'

Mention of the Enchanter had an immediate effect upon the Smugweeds. They began to tremble and backed away from Sophie and Felicity.

'Do you speak truth? Do you know him?' asked one, voice quivering.

'We do!' said Sophie, before Felicity could speak. 'In fact, the Enchanter is *her* grandfather and he'll be *very* annoyed when he finds out you've captured his only granddaughter – and her best friend.'

'It's true,' added Felicity. 'But free us, and we'll say nothing about it. We're trying to find him, actually, so if you know where he is, or how we might get to him, we'd be very appreciative.' She paused. 'So would my grandfather – and my mother and grandmother.'

The Smugweeds whispered between themselves for a while as Felicity and Sophie looked on. At last, they appeared to be decided and approached the girls.

'The Enchanter and his family have just recently helped to save the realm,' said one Smugweed, 'so if you are truly part of that family then we are grateful and glad and we will help you.'

'So they're safe?' said Felicity with relief. 'We've been separated, you see. The last I knew was that they had been captured by the witches.'

'Yes,' said the other Smugweed. 'Captured, but strong enough together to defeat the witches from within. As the realm healed and the darkness drained away from it, the witches found themselves in trouble.'

'Trouble, yes,' chipped in the other Smugweed, each seeming now to relish the storytelling. 'The Enchanter and enchantresses used magic within—'

'The Fairy King and Queen used their magic from without—'

'With armies—'

'Of spell-casters—'

'Conjurors—'

'Wizards—'

'Elves—'

'Not Smugweeds, though.'

'We hid—'

'And hoped—'

'Then heard—'

'We heard the news and saw the signs. We watched the sky and listened to the ocean's cries.'

'Then we saw a phoenix fly in with the dawn and took it as a special sign.'

'We shot you down—'

'And here we are.'

Everyone looked at one another.

'That's a wonderful story!' said Sophie. 'So, er, can you please untie us now? We promise we won't run away.'

The Smugweeds hesitated, then untied the girls and backed away from them, as if afraid of what they might do.

'We won't harm you,' said Felicity. 'And thank you. Now, let's see about getting us back to my family.'

***

The Smugweeds didn't have very much magic to speak of, but what they did have was really all that they – and Felicity and Sophie – needed in the end. They could converse with their relatives from the ocean - those who remained tethered to the tides – and so, passed their message into the waves.

From there, it moved from aquatic plant to aquatic plant – a wave of words travelling far and wide – until at last, it reached the river-dwelling plants, heading upstream to a place where ears which understood the rhythms of nature perked up and relayed it on to where it needed to go.

In the cave, at the cove, with the Smugweeds, Felicity and Sophie waited.

Chapter Thirty
Per Aspera ad Astra

When night brushed across the horizon and stars dusted the sky, Felicity looked up and wondered where the Riddler was in that cosmic mass, and what he was getting up to. Free to pursue his dreams at last – no longer just looking at worlds within worlds – she was curious as to whether he would now be satisfied, or if he would always be seeking that which was just beyond his grasp.

It felt odd to be waiting, not doing, for a change, but she had to admit she was glad of the rest and was thankful their adventuring seemed to be drawing to a close. She knew now what her Granny Stone meant when she said that a person could have 'too much of a good thing' sometimes. Adventuring certainly wasn't easy, but she *did* enjoy the thrill of it and had always yearned for it.

Felicity definitely felt that she'd had enough excitement for a while, however, though she knew that life was never dull in the Fairy Realm, nor, if you took the time to stop and look, in the Human Realm either.

She still wondered about what hidden gifts she might possess, but was prepared to wait for those, if indeed she really had any, and to learn what she could from her family. She knew better than anyone that you didn't need to possess magic to have magical experiences.

The Smugweeds had relaxed a little more around them as the day wore on, and now night had draped itself across the realm again, they were outside scavenging for their treasures while Felicity and Sophie watched on the sand. They were in the middle of chatting about all their adventures again when someone dropped down beside Felicity. Someone else appeared at Sophie's side and they both jumped. Then Felicity grinned.

'Bob! And – Butterkin? You're back – and changed!'

The brownies grinned right back at Felicity and Sophie.

'Well – where did you two disappear to?' asked Sophie with a smile. 'We ended up stranded in a witch tower in a forest, and then I turned into a phoenix and flew us over Fairyland, only to be struck down by *those* two.' She pointed at the Smugweeds a little way off. 'Although, being a phoenix was pretty awesome.'

'We have a bit of a story to tell too,' said Bob. 'We were whisked away to my house, as planned, but we weren't there five minutes before there was a rap on the door and who should we find on the threshold but a very weary and worried-looking Enchanter and his wife and daughter!'

'Yes, we had barely caught our breath,' said Butterkin. 'But we explained everything – well, Bob did – and then the Enchanter, tired though he was, did a spell to turn me back into a brownie, although he seems to think that I might regain my Glider form if I'm ever out in a misty night …'

'We could have some fun with *that*,' said Bob, eyes twinkling. 'Anyway, as Butterkin said, we explained what we could, but we *couldn't* explain where you'd gone to after we used the Causeway stones, as we'd all expected to arrive at my house.

'Your family suspected the witches had laid a trap for you, Felicity, should you return from the Mountain of Lore. The Enchanter was very surprised, by the way, to learn that it was in "The Deep", and that we all went there! I told them about you too, Sophie, and they seemed glad that Felicity had had two friends with her along the way. But, I digress.'

'It's true, then, what the Smugweeds said?' Felicity interrupted. 'The realm is back to normal again?'

Bob nodded. 'Well, almost. The borders have healed and closed again – we got everyone back who was lost, thanks to the extra help from those we found along the way – so that helped a great deal. It prevented more dark magic from seeping in, and many creatures fled back to their homes when they realised what was happening and that they would be trapped here, while others were captured by the Royal Army.'

'There are still some creatures unaccounted for,' added Butterkin, 'but on the whole, Fairyland is re-stitched and revived!'

The friends all grinned at one another.

'So, now what?' asked Sophie.

'Now, we take you back to the Mystical Mansion – and to Felicity's family – then I suppose you will go home, Sophie, and Felicity …?'

'I will stay here,' she said, eyes gleaming. 'Though I *will* visit, Soph. And I'm sure the Enchanter can find, or conjure up, some sort of magic mirror, so we can do the Fairyland equivalent of Skype!'

'I'll miss you, Felicity, but I'd say we have a deal,' said Sophie. 'We'll need to keep those lines of communication well open though, because I have a *lot* of stuff to process and I'll go mad at home otherwise, with no one to talk to about it all!'

'Agreed,' said Felicity with a smile.

The Smugweeds had spotted the brownies and came up to say their goodbyes, then Bob and Butterkin took Felicity and Sophie by the hands and muttered the spell the Enchanter had told them to say. When the final syllable had been uttered, they vanished from the cove.

***

Felicity felt her feet touch down on solid ground in what felt like the blink of an eye, but which she knew, of course, was the flash of magic. She let go of her friends' hands and spun round as she heard a mixture of familiar voices behind her.

'*Felicitina*!' boomed the Enchanter in delight, as he approached with her mum and Granny Stone, all swirling cloak and coiffed black hair, still streaked with silver. Felicity also spied Hatchet behind them, looking at her with a big grin on his sharp-featured hobgoblin face. 'Good to have you home again.' The Enchanter winked at her and she smiled.

Yes, thought Felicity. It was good to be home.

And so, we must leave Felicity Stone,
Or Felicitina, as she now will be known.
A girl who solved riddles and restored pebble magic -
One who saved Fairyland from something quite tragic.
She met Gobblers, nymphs and sea creatures galore,
Gliders, a Moon Hare – things none saw before.
A brownie called Bob who became a great friend –
He was there from the start, he'll be there till the end.
They journeyed far, to the depths of the sea,
After whispering trees and, of course, Sophie.
In this hidden world they had to explore,
Uncovering the Riddler at the Mountain of Lore.
Whisked through the cosmos, not a moment too soon,
They defeated the mist with the light of the moon.
Fairyland's borders re-stitched and re-healed,
Darkness was banished, the realm once more sealed.
Of course, creatures unsavoury linger there still,
They always have and they always will.
But, as Felicity learned – magic or not –
The best way to succeed is to use what you've got.
In the Fairy Realm, there she has stayed,
Though from time-to-time, a visit is paid …
To a world that is human, through and through,
Yet it has its own magic – this much is true.
You can spot it yourself, in the curl of a fern,
In the song of the ocean, in the voice of a tern.
It's carried along in the wind and the rain …
Once you find it, there's magic, again and again.

Acknowledgements

Thanks to …
The Arts Council of Northern Ireland,
in particular, to Damian Smyth.
Also, to Kelly Creighton, Kerry McLean,
Andrew Brown, Averill Buchanan,
my family,
&
to you, for joining Felicity on her second adventure in
the Fairy Realm.

Author's note

If, like myself, you were glued to the screen when the BBC aired Blue Planet II, then you might recognise some of the seascape which appears in *Phantom Phantasia*.

Indeed, it was while watching one of the earlier episodes, entitled 'The Deep', that I decided I wanted Felicity to journey underwater to discover the wonderfully magical realm that exists just out of sight, beneath the waves. It is beautiful, mysterious and rich with spectacular marine life, yet also dark, dangerous and eerie. There's everything from monster waves, black holes and the Pools of Despair, to the kelp forests, marine meadows and saltwater trees which are collectively called the 'Blue Forests'.

Very few people have explored the deepest part of the ocean – the Challenger Deep – and we are only just beginning to discover what lies in these hidden depths. However, scientists have now identified various zones to help differentiate the deep sea, including the sunlight, twilight and midnight zones.

Next, comes the Abyssal Realm (renamed in *Phantom Phantasia* as the Abysmal Realm), followed by the Challenger Deep at the very bottom - a place resplendent in ocean trenches, enchanted/coral gardens, submarine canyons, rift valleys, hills, active underwater volcanoes, and mountains - including the sprawling Mid-Ocean Ridge.

There is a world of wonder concealed beneath the waves and I've woven some of these marvellous things into my story. I've done this because they're amazing, but also, because I hope it will remind readers that we have a wealth of biodiversity in the sea which might be out of sight, but should never be out of mind.

So, what you've just read is a mixture of the magical and real-life. I've taken some creative licence with aspects of my underwater kingdom – for example, in Fairyland, species can, thanks to magic, thrive beyond their more natural habitats, so some are a little displaced. However, Bobbits and sea-angels really do exist, and giant Leatherback turtles have been known to stray into the colder waters around the north coast of Ireland, where I live. I can't vouch for the existence of the Mountain of Lore, but who knows …?

The ocean is really rather wonderful. Let's keep it that way.

About the Author

Claire Savage grew up deep in the countryside around Magherafelt, Northern Ireland, where she spent lots of time reading stories of magic and adventure. Like Felicity, she wanted to enjoy her own exciting escapades, so often went exploring with her brothers and sister – and a fair few cats – in the surrounding fields and lanes.

Holidays were spent on the North Coast, where she now lives and walks every day with her cocker spaniel, Reuben, getting lots of inspiration from both the sea and landscape.

Claire works as a copywriter and journalist by day, but by night, she can more usually be found conjuring up strange and unusual tales …

In November 2017, Claire received a General Arts Award from the Arts Council Northern Ireland's National Lottery fund to support her artistic production, the writing of *Phantom Phantasia* and to further assist in creating a support structure for *Magical Masquerade*. Claire received a similar award in July 2014, when a National Lottery grant from the Arts Council NI's Support for Individual Artists Programme backed her in writing a collection of short stories and poetry.

In 2016, Claire was chosen as one of Lagan Online's 12NOW (New Original Writers) for 2016/17.

A variety of Claire's short stories have been published in literary journals, including *The Lonely Crowd*, *The Incubator*, *The Launchpad* and *The Ghastling*, as well as in *SHIFT Lit - Derry* writing magazine, with some poetry also in print.

When she isn't writing, Claire loves reading all sorts of books (and scouring bookshops for new titles), spending time with Reuben, baking, and daydreaming. She also enjoys hosting the Giant's Causeway Book Club, which was launched in June 2018.

Phantom Phantasia is Claire's second novel and the sequel to *Magical Masquerade*, which launched at the Belfast Book Festival 2017. It was also part of Derry's SBOOKY Festival 2017 and the Dublin Book Festival 2017.

Author blog: *www.clairesavagewriting.wordpress.com/*
Facebook: *Claire Savage - Author*
Twitter: *@ClaireLSavage*